Sharon Raunworth

॥║▌║▌║║▌║║▌║║║▌║▌║║║▌▌║║▌
◁ **W9-BAL-837**

What readers say about Harlequin Romances

"Your books are the best I have ever found."
P.B.*, Bellevue, Washington

"I enjoy them more and more
with each passing year."
J.L., Spurlockville, West Virginia

"No matter how full and happy life might be,
it is an enchantment to sit
and read your novels."
D.K., Willowdale, Ontario

"I firmly believe that Harlequin Romances
are perfect for anyone who wants to read
a good romance."
C.R., Akron, Ohio

*Names available on request

OTHER
Harlequin Romances
by BETTY NEELS

Many of these titles are available at your local bookseller
or through the Harlequin Reader Service.

For a free catalogue listing all available Harlequin Romances,
send your name and address to:

HARLEQUIN READER SERVICE,
M.P.O. Box 707, Niagara Falls, N.Y. 14302
Canadian address: Stratford, Ontario, Canada N5A 6W4

or use order coupon at back of books.

A Matter of Chance

by

BETTY NEELS

Harlequin Books

TORONTO • LONDON • NEW YORK • AMSTERDAM • SYDNEY

Original hardcover edition published in 1977
by Mills & Boon Limited

ISBN 0-373-02095-3

Harlequin edition published August 1977

Copyright © 1977 by Betty Neels. All rights reserved.
Except for use in any review, the reproduction or utilization of this
work in whole or in part in any form by any electronic, mechanical
or other means, now known or hereafter invented, including xero-
graphy, photocopying and recording, or in any information storage or
retrieval system, is forbidden without the permission of the publisher.
All the characters in this book have no existence outside the imagination of the author and have no relation whatsoever to anyone bearing
the same name or names. They are not even distantly inspired by
any individual known or unknown to the author, and all the incidents
are pure invention.

The Harlequin trademark, consisting of the word HARLEQUIN and the
portrayal of a Harlequin, is registered in the United States Patent
Office and in the Canada Trade Marks Office.

Printed in U.S.A.

CHAPTER ONE

CRESSIDA BINGLEY stood at the corner of a narrow, dingy street in the heart of Amsterdam and knew that she was lost—temporarily at least. She peered at the map she was holding without much success; the October afternoon was darkening, so that to study it was fruitless. She tried to remember in which direction she had walked from the Dam Square, but the city was built like a spider's web with canals for its threads, and she had wandered aimlessly, looking around her without noting her whereabouts. She bent her head and peered down once more, but the long, foreign names, only half seen in the gathering dusk, eluded her; she was frowning over them when someone spoke behind her and she almost dropped the map. Presumably she had been addressed in Dutch, for she hadn't understood a word. She sighed, for this was the third time that afternoon that a man had stopped and spoken to her; she had been polite with the first one, a little impatient with the second, but now she was vexed. She turned sharply and said in a cold voice, 'I can't understand you, so do go away!'

Her voice died as she saw him; he towered over her own five feet eight inches by at least another eight inches. But it wasn't only his height, he was large, too, blocking her way, and even in the poor light she could see that he was handsome, with a nose which dominated his face, its flared nostrils giving it an air of arrogance. She couldn't see the colour of his eyes, but the brows above them were winged and as pale as his hair. He wasn't quite smiling, his mouth had a mocking quirk, that was all.

'English,' he observed, 'and telling me to go away when you're lost.' His deep voice mocked her, just as his smile did, and it annoyed her.

'I am not lost,' she protested untruthfully. 'I stopped to look at the map ... there is no need for you ...'

A large, gloved hand took the map from her grasp and turned it right side up. 'Try it that way,' he suggested, 'and unless you are quite sure where you are, even in the dark, I suggest you put your pride in your pocket and let me show you the way— it will be night in another ten minutes, and,' he added blandly, 'this isn't a part of Amsterdam which tourists frequent—certainly not young women such as yourself, at any rate.'

She could hear the amusement behind the blandness and her annoyance sharpened even while she had to admit that she was lost. The street was empty too, and even if someone came along they might not understand her; she would be at a disadvantage. She said stiffly: 'If you would direct me to the Rembrandt Plein—I can find my way from there.'

He looked down at her, smiling quite openly

now. 'Very well. Go to the end of this street on your left, turn right and take the second turning on the right— there's a narrow lane half way down which will bring you out into a small square which has five streets leading from it—take the one with the tobacconist's shop on the corner; you'll find the Rembrandt Plein at the end of it.'

Cressida shot him a cold look. 'I think I'll do better if I find my own way, thank you, though I'm sure you mean to be kind ...'

He shook his head. 'I'm seldom that,' he assured her placidly, 'but I intend to take you as far as the Rembrandt Plein—it isn't far and I know all the short cuts.' He added silkily: 'You can always scream.'

The thought had crossed her mind too, so that she said very emphatically: 'I have no intention of doing any such thing; I'm very well able to look after myself.'

He smiled again and began to walk briskly down the street he had pointed out to her, and after a moment or so, made a few desultory remarks about Amsterdam and the weather, adding the kind of questions usually asked of tourists: had she seen the Dam Palace, Rembrandt's House, the Rijksmuseum ... She answered briefly, intent on keeping pace with his long stride, managing to steal a glance or two at him as they went. He was older than she had first supposed, well into his thirties, she would imagine, and dressed with a quiet elegance which, for some reason, reassured her. If they hadn't started off on the wrong foot, she thought belatedly, she could have asked him where he lived—what he did ... 'Am I taking you out of your way?' she asked suddenly.

She got an uncompromising 'Yes,' and he added, 'but it's of no importance,' and at that moment they turned a corner and she saw the Rembrandt Plein not many yards away. 'I'm sorry,' she said stiffly. 'I must have taken up your time—I know where I am now.' She came to a halt. 'Good night, and thank you.'

'Don't be silly,' he spoke with amused impatience. 'Where is your hotel?'

Rather to her own surprise, she told him quite meekly, and fell into step beside him again while he crossed the square, its cafés and clubs still half empty before the evening crowds arrived, and took another narrow street on its opposite side.

'This isn't the way,' said Cressida, and stopped again.

'A short cut. My dear good girl, when will you realise that I am merely seeing you to your hotel as quickly as possible, and am not bent on getting to know you—picking you up is the expression, I believe.'

If she had known where to go, she would have left him then and there, but she didn't. She walked beside him, too furious to speak, until the street turned at right angles and opened into the broad street running beside a canal where her hotel was. At its door she wished him a chilly good night, offered even chillier thanks, and whisked herself in through its narrow door. The chilliness was wasted on him, though, for he laughed softly and didn't say a word. He was detestable, she told herself, as she ran up the precipitous stairs to the top floor.

The hotel was small and narrow, supported on either side by equally small and narrow houses—hotels too—a dozen of them in a neat row, with immaculate curtains at their shining windows and semi-basement dining rooms where their guests breakfasted, and where they could, if they wished, have a snack in the evening. Cressida reached the top floor and went down the passage with its rows of doors. Her room was at the end, small, spotlessly clean and pleasantly warm. It was almost six o'clock. In half an hour she would go all the way downstairs again and have coffee and a *broodje* and then come back and pack her bag, but now she sat on the bed, still in her coat, suddenly doubtful about everything. If someone had told her two weeks ago that she would be staying in an Amsterdam hotel, en route for a job in Friesland, she would have laughed at the very idea, yet here she was—and looking back, she wondered at the quirk of fate which had hurried her along towards it, making everything so easy and giving her no time to think until she was here ... she took off her coat and started to unpin her hair and then sat brushing it, while she brooded about her future.

Her hair was fine and silky and very dark, hanging down to her waist. Her brows were dark too, thick and well shaped above large brown eyes, generously lashed. Her nose was small and straight and her mouth curved delightfully—a beautiful face, and she had a figure to match it. But although she was staring at her reflection in the small wall mirror, she didn't really see it. 'I must be mad,' she said out loud, and quite forgetful of her hair, put down the brush and did nothing at all while she looked back over the last week or so. Not too far back; she still couldn't think of her father's death and then her mother's so soon after without a deep grief which threatened to engulf her. Her father had been ill for only a few days; visiting a parishioner with 'flu, he had fallen a victim to it himself, and while the parishioner recovered, her father had died, and then, within a week, her mother, leaving her alone and desolate but with little time for grief, for the rectory had to be vacated, the furniture sold and a few modest debts paid, and when that was done, there was very little money over.

It had been a wrench to leave the village in Dorset where she had spent her childhood and all her holidays since she had taken up nursing; she had gathered together a few of her parents' most loved bits and pieces, packed her clothes, and gone to stay with her mother's elder sister, a small, bustling woman who lived alone in a minuscule thatched cottage on the edge of a village in the same county. It was while she was there that she decided to give up her job at the big London hospital where she was Sister of a medical ward, and until she could make up her mind about her future, take private cases. And Aunt Emily had agreed; change, she had observed wisely, was absolutely essential when one had been dealt such a severe blow—and time, time to think about the future and come to terms with it. She thought privately that Cressida would certainly marry later on, once the icy grief which held her fast had thawed a little and she could laugh again and enjoy meeting people. But that was something she couldn't tell her niece; all she could do was to tell her to regard the overcrowded little cottage as her home and know that she was welcome there.

A couple of weeks' peace and quiet had helped Cressida a great deal. Armed with excellent references and a resolve to make a new life for herself, she went up to London and presented herself at an agency highly recommended by her hospital. The temptation to take the first job offered to her was great, but she still had a little money, enough to stay in a rather seedy hotel for a week, until a case turned up which would appeal to her, so she rejected the first few offered to her; a child film star with tonsillitis, a young drug addict, a wealthy widow who really wanted a slave, not a nurse. After the third day she wondered if she was being unduly fussy; some of the girls she met there came in, accepted a case, and were away again in five minutes. But there was another girl who was choosy too— Molly, a small, fair creature with a sweet, rather weak face, who confided to Cressida that she was waiting for a job as far away as possible because she had quarrelled with her fiancé and never wanted to see him again. It was towards the end of the week when she told Cressida that she had got a job, and not through the agency. 'My uncle got it for me; at least, this doctor asked him to find a nurse who could type, and I can. You see, he's writing a book and he needs an English girl—a nurse who'll understand the medical terms—so that she can help him with the English and type it too—and he lives in Holland, so I can get away from Jim.'

She skipped away in great good spirits, leaving Cressida to make the difficult choice between a case of delirium tremens and an elderly lady who wanted someone to see her through the brief trials of having all her teeth out. Cressida decided against them both, was treated to a brief homily by the agency clerk on being too fussy, and left in her turn, to walk in St James's Park and wish that the months could roll back and she could be on her way home for her holidays. She walked on steadily; she wasn't going to cry, she told herself firmly, not in the middle of a public park, at any rate. She had sat down on a bench and made a great business of feeding the birds with the sandwiches she had brought with her for lunch and didn't want.

She hadn't seen Molly on the following morning and hadn't expected to; probably she was on her way to Holland already. Waiting her turn, she promised herself that she would take the first case she was offered, but when she got into the office the clerk said briskly: 'Sorry, there's nothing today—if you'd been here half an hour earlier I could have fixed you up ... Better luck tomorrow.'

She smiled her bright, meaningless smile and

12

Cressida smiled back, not sure if she was relieved or not. She was standing in the agency entrance, trying to make up her mind what to do with her empty day, when Molly came dashing towards her.

'I hoped I'd find you,' she cried breathlessly. 'I've a whole lot to tell you and it'll take a minute or two. There's a café down the street, come and have some coffee.'

'You've made it up with your Jim,' declared Cressida.

Molly caught her by the arm. 'Yes, I have, isn't it super? But that isn't all.'

She had dragged Cressida down the street towards the café. 'That job—the one I said I'd take in Holland—well, I can't go now, can I? I mean, Jim wants us to get married straight away—so I thought of you ...' She had paused maddeningly as they entered the café, found a table and ordered coffee. 'You can type, you told me so—and the job is about the alimentary system and its disorders, and you've had a medical ward ... don't you see? It's just made for you.'

'But I can't,' said Cressida. 'I don't know this doctor and he doesn't know me.'

Molly opened her handbag and dragged out a small pile of letters. 'Here are all the letters so's you can see that it really is a job—and my uncle says if you could go and see him—he lives in Hampstead, he's got a practice there—this afternoon after surgery ...' She had sugared her coffee and continued: 'Oh, you must! You wanted something interesting and different, didn't you? Uncle says it would take about six or seven weeks, and the pay's good. At least go and see my uncle.'

And Cressida had said yes quickly before she could change her mind.

Molly's uncle had been nice; elderly and a little slow, and although he had asked her a great many questions, he had been so nice about it that she hadn't minded answering them. 'It seems to me,' he told her finally, 'that this job is just what you need. I appreciate your need to get away, Miss Bingley, and Doctor van Blom is most anxious to find someone who can type adequately as well as give him occasional help with the turn of a phrase and so on.' He smiled kindly. 'May I take it that you will help him out?'

Cressida had said that yes, she would like to very much, but she would have to get her passport renewed and pack a few things. He had nodded and said, 'Quite —could you be ready in four or five days' time?'

They had made their arrangements there and then, but it was Cressida who had decided to leave two days earlier and spend them in Amsterdam. One of her friends at the hospital gave her the name of the hotel and she had had no difficulty in getting a room.

She had spent her two days exploring the city, spending hours in the museums, walking endlessly beside the canals, looking at the old houses which lined their banks, eating frugally at lunch bars, and window-shopping. And now, in the morning, she would catch a train to Leeuwarden where she would be met.

She glanced at the clock and began to coil her hair rapidly; the dining room was only open for a short time each evening; the hotel guests were expected to dine out, the snacks were for those who had just arrived, or who, for some reason or other, were going to spend their evening in their rooms.

There was a very small room by the entrance where one could get a drink or coffee, but Cressida had never seen anyone in it. She did her face and washed her hands and went down the staircase once more, to the basement, where she sat down at a table for one, drank the coffee she ordered and ate two ham rolls. They were excellent, but she had very little appetite. Indeed, she had grown thin during the last few weeks; meals, like so many other things, had become just something to get through as best she might. She supposed that in time everything would be normal again, as the incoming rector had assured her when he had called to make himself known to her and arrange to move into the rectory. Time he had said, healed everything, and she hadn't disputed that fact; only time, when it lay heavy, took a long time to pass.

She went back to her room presently and packed her case, had a shower in the cramped cabinet down the passage, and got into bed. She wasn't sleepy, but bed gave an illusion of cosiness. She had a sudden, vivid memory of the sitting room in her old home, with a log fire blazing in the hearth and the shabby armchairs pulled close to it, and for a moment she couldn't see the map she was studying for the tears in her eyes, but she brushed them away resolutely and applied herself once more to its perusal. Molly's uncle had told her that Doctor van Blom lived in a village between Groningen and Leeuwarden, he had told her the name too, but the two cities were thirty miles apart and from the numerous villages between, not one of their peculiar-looking names rang a bell of recognition. She would have to wait and see.

The tram Cressida took to the station in the morning was packed with early morning workers, but the train, when she eventually found the right platform and caught it by the skin of her teeth, was almost empty. She sat in her corner seat, watching the small flat fields give way to the woods and heaths of the Veluwe and then fields again, but now they had become wide and rolling and the towns less frequent. She had chosen to go via Groningen, and that city, when the train reached it, looked invitingly picturesque as well as large and bustling. As the train pulled away from the station she craned her neck to see the last of its spires and towers and then turned to look at the countryside with some eagerness. Somewhere close by was the village where she was to spend the next few weeks. She stared at the strange names on the station boards as they passed, but both Dutch and Friesian names were quite incomprehensible to her. However, she had been told not to worry about the language; Doctor van Blom spoke excellent English and the people she would meet would have a sufficient knowledge of it to make her lack of Dutch no problem at all.

She got out at Leeuwarden station with much the same feeling as she experienced when she entered a dentist's surgery; her future employer might be bad-tempered, impatient, a slave-driver ... She stood under the clock on the platform as she had been told to do, and looked around her, and a great many people looked back at her, for she was quite eye-catching, her beautiful face pale with excitement and apprehension, her nicely cut tweed coat showing off her slenderness to perfection, the brown fur hat perched on top of her shining bun of hair highlighting its vivid darkness.

She didn't have to wait long; from the people around her there emerged a short, stout man in his late middle years. He came straight at her, beaming all over his nice round face, beginning to talk to her long before he reached her. 'Miss Bingley—Miss Cressida Bingley—what a charming name! I am delighted to welcome you; you see that I knew you at once.' He was pumping her arm up and down as he spoke. 'My old friend Doctor Mills described you so well ... you have luggage with you? This case only? Then we will go to the car at once and return to my home as quickly as possible. We will drink coffee together and talk of my book which I am so anxious to complete.'

He walked as he talked, his hand on her arm, edging her towards the station entrance where a splendidly kept dark blue Chevrolet stood. He ushered her into the front seat, put her luggage in the boot and got into the driving seat. 'Fifteen of your English miles,' he observed, 'we shall be there very shortly.'

But not as shortly as all that, Cressida discovered. They drove very slowly through the city, a busy, bustling place she wanted to explore, and she wondered if there was something about Dutch motoring laws she didn't know—a twenty-mile speed limit in towns, for instance, and yet everyone else was travelling twice as fast. Perhaps her new employer was just a very cautious driver. On the outskirts of Leeuwarden he achieved a steady thirty, while cars flashed past at thrice that speed and Cressida, who in happier times had driven her father's car rather well, longed to stretch out a neatly booted foot and slam it down on the accelerator, for it seemed to her a crying shame to own such a powerful car and not make use of it. She kept her itching foot still and watched the slowly passing scenery while she answered her companion's stream of questions. Even if he was a shocking driver, he was rather an old dear.

They turned off the main road presently and trickled cautiously down a narrow lane. 'Eestrum,' the doctor informed her as they approached and passed through a smallish village. 'We go to Augustinusga, that is where I live, so well placed between Leeuwarden and Gronigen. It is convenient for me —and my partners—to travel to either place.'

'Partners?' asked Cressida. No one had mentioned them.

'Doctor Herrima—we share a house and a house-

18

keeper—and Doctor van der Teile, who is the senior partner and does not live in the village. We consult him, you understand; all the more difficult cases, but for the most of the time he is either at Leeuwarden or Groningen, for he has beds in both hospitals as well as consulting rooms. He is a distinguished physician and travels a good deal.'

Cressida murmured politely; he would be a very elderly man, she imagined, for Doctor van Blom was certainly in his sixties and this other partner was the senior ... the third partner would be the youngest and the junior. The three bears; she suppressed a giggle.

Her companion had dropped the car's speed to a smart walking pace and began pointing out local landmarks. A windmill, standing lonely in the wintry fields by a canal, a little wood on the other side of the water, bare and dull in the morning's grey bleakness, but, she was assured, a charming place in the spring. An austere red brick church with plain glass windows came into view and a cosy little house beside it. 'The *dominee* and his wife live there,' explained Doctor van Blom. 'A good friend of ours, and here, at the beginning of the village, is an excellent example of our Friesian farms.'

Cressida was still craning her neck to see the last of it as they entered the village itself, circled the square lined with houses and stopped cautiously outside one of them, a red brick house with its door exactly in the centre and its windows arranged across its face in mathematical rows. She hoped it wasn't as plain inside as it was out, and had her hope realised; the front door opened on to a long, narrow hall, lofty-ceilinged and a little dark and from which numerous doors opened. Doctor van Blom threw open the first of these and ushered her in, at the same time raising his voice in a mild bellow. This was instantly answered in person by his housekeeper, a tall, thin woman, no longer young but with such a forceful air about her that one could have imagined her barely in her prime. She smiled at the doctor, smiled at Cressida, shook her hand and followed them into what was obviously the sitting-room, comfortably furnished, the leather chairs a little shabby perhaps, but there was some beautiful china and silver lying around on shelves and tables, rather as though someone had just been admiring the objects and set them down haphazardly. There were shelves of books, too, and an old-fashioned stove giving off a most welcome heat.

Cressida took the chair she was offered and surrendered her coat to the housekeeper, her unhappy heart much cheered by her kindly reception, and when Juffrouw Naald went away and came back a moment later with a tray laden with coffee-cups and biscuits, she partook of these refreshments with more pleasure that she had felt for some time.

They had been sitting for perhaps ten minutes when the door opened and a tall, thin man, about the same age as Doctor van Blom, came in. 'My partner, Doctor Herrima,' her employer told her, and after introductions had been made, Cressida found herself sitting between the two of them, filling their coffee-cups and answering their gentle questions.

'A pretty girl,' observed Doctor Herrima to no one in particular, 'a very pretty girl.' He looked keenly at her. 'And you can type, I understand?'

She assured him that she could.

'You are also a nurse?'

'Oh, yes,' she told him, 'I've been trained for more than four years.'

He looked across at his partner. 'A splendid choice.' And when his partner nodded happily, 'What do you think of our country, Miss Bingley?'

Cressida put down her cup. 'Well, I haven't seen a great deal of it. Two days in Amsterdam and then coming here by train ...'

'You must see Leeuwarden and Groningen—now there are two magnificent centuries-old cities. Do you drive?' It was Doctor van Blom who spoke.

'Yes—we had a rather elderly Morris.'

'Ah.' He pondered this for a minute. 'My car is a powerful one, as you may have noticed, and Doctor Herrima runs a BMW. I do not know if you feel competent to drive either of them?' He sounded doubtful.

Cressida thought of the snail-like pace at which they had driven from Leeuwarden and replied soberly that she thought she would be capable of driving either of the cars. Indeed, the idea of driving the Chev on one of the excellent motorways appealed to her very much: to drive and drive and drive, away from her grief and loneliness.

She shut her mind to the idea and made a

suitably admiring remark about the car, to which Doctor van Blom responded with instant eagerness. They were two dears, she decided; unworldly and content in their rather cluttered, pleasant sitting-room.

She asked diffidently about their practice and was told at some length and sometimes twice over that it was a large one, covering a great number of outlying villages and farms; that they had a baby clinic once a week, a small surgery for emergencies, and dealt with a wide variety of patients.

'There are quite a number of accidents,' explained Doctor van Blom, 'farms, you know—they have these modern machines, some of them are complicated and if a farm worker doesn't understand what he is doing ...' He gave a little shrug. 'And then of course there are those who live some way away, and they tend to delay sending for us or coming to the surgery, and sometimes the injury or illness is made much worse in consequence. We have splendid hospitals, of course, and our senior partner is always available for consultation.' He wagged his balding head. 'A very clever man,' he stated, 'as well as our great friend. He had an English godfather, and you will find his English excellent.'

Cressida dismissed this paragon with a nice smile and asked about the book. 'When would you like me to start?' she wanted to know.

'You feel that you could start today? Splendid, Miss Bingley—perhaps after lunch?'

'That would be fine, and please will you call me Cressida?'

They both beamed at her. 'With pleasure. And now you would like to go to your room and unpack. We have lunch at noon—is that time enough for you to settle in?'

They escorted her to the door, cried in unison for Juffrouw Naald, and stood watching her as she trod up the steep, uncarpeted stairs to the floor above, with the housekeeper leading the way.

Her room was in the front of the house, a corner room with big windows so that she had a wide view of the square below and the houses around it. It was nicely furnished if a trifle heavily, with Second Empire mahogany bed, matching chest of drawers, a ponderous dressing table and an enormous clothes closet. There was a small easy chair by the window and a writing table and a little shelf of books. Leading from it was a well-appointed bathroom; after the tiny room in Aunt Emily's cottage, it seemed like luxury to Cressida. Someone had put chrysanthemums in a vase by the bed too; she smiled and touched them and looked at Juffrouw Naald who smiled and nodded and said something Cressida couldn't understand, but it sounded friendly.

When the housekeeper had gone, Cressida unpacked quickly, tidied her hair and did her face and repaired downstairs, to find both doctors waiting for her.

'We drink Jenever, but for you we have sherry—shall we take a glass now before lunch? You are hungry?'

They both stood looking at her with eager kindness and she hastened to assure them that she was —a pleasant sensation after weeks of not bothering what she ate. She accompanied them into the dining-room, a lofty apartment, furnished with mahogany as solid as her bedroom was and with a crimson carpet underfoot and crimson curtains at its windows, a suitable background for the snow-white tablecloth and shining silver. The meal was a simple one; the doctors, they assured her, liked their dinner in the evening after surgery, but she found the soup, dish of cold meats and the basket of various breads more than sufficient. There was no surgery that afternoon, she was told, so that there was no need for them to hurry over their meal, and after it she and Doctor van Blom could retire to his study while Doctor Herrima did the afternoon round. If he explained his work, suggested the doctor, perhaps she might make a start on sorting out the manuscript and preparing it for typing? She could have the evening too, while he took surgery. He passed his cup for more coffee and while she was pouring it, the door opened and in walked the man who had taken her back to her hotel in Amsterdam the day before. Cressida put down the coffee-pot carefully, and with the cup and saucer still in her hand, sat staring at him, her pretty mouth very slightly open.

'Giles,' boomed Doctor van Blom, 'what good fortune—now you can meet the young lady who is to help me with my book—Miss Cressida Bingley.' He waved a hand. 'Cressida, this is our senior partner, Doctor van der Teile.'

He closed the door after him and crossed over to her chair. 'You look surprised,' he observed blandly.

'Well, I am ... I didn't expect ...'

'No? But my dear girl, it was inevitable.' He took the cup and saucer from her, handed it across the table to his partner and pulled out a chair for himself. 'Cressida and I have already met,' he told his partners, and when the fresh coffee came, accepted a cup before asking her, in the politest manner possible, if she would forgive him if he discussed a case with his partners.

And if that isn't a hint to make myself scarce, I don't know what is, thought Cressida. She gave him a haughty look and got up at once. 'I have my unpacking to finish,' she assured him, and sailed to the door, only to find him there to open it for her.

'I'll be gone very shortly,' he murmured as she went past him. 'You can safely come down again in half an hour.'

CHAPTER TWO

DOCTOR VAN DER TEILE had gone by the time Cressida, rather uncertain as to what was expected of her, went downstairs again, but Doctor van Blom put his head round a door as she reached the hall, obviously on the lookout for her, and invited her to enter his study.

'No time like the present,' he assured her with the air of a man who had just thought up a clever remark, and ushered her in. Compared with the sitting-room it was quite small, furnished with a large desk with a leather chair behind it, a pair of similar chairs on either side of the stove, and a smaller desk against one wall with a typewriter on it. The walls were lined with vast quantities of books; Cressida, who liked reading, promised herself a good browse through them when the opportunity occurred, but now she sat down in the chair opposite the doctor's and gave him her full attention.

Would she mind working early in the morning? he wanted to know anxiously—before surgery started at eight o'clock. He himself was an early riser and had formed the habit of putting in an hour's work before breakfast, which was at half past seven each day except Sunday.

Cressida paled a little at the prospect of rising at six o'clock each morning; she had no objection to getting up early and it was a job, after all, which she was being paid for, but surely the hour was a bit much? She caught her companion's eye fixed pleadingly on her, and heard herself say cheerfully that she didn't mind in the least, wondering at the same time how long her working day was to be.

She was enlightened almost at once. 'If you could work on your own during surgery,' went on the doctor. 'We have coffee about ten o'clock, before we do our rounds; if you would like to take an hour's break then and afterwards continue working until we have our lunch? The afternoon surgery is at half past one—if you would work until we go on our afternoon visits. You could be free then until we have a cup of tea on our return—about half past four. We might do another hour's work together until evening surgery starts. We dine at half past seven ...' He cast her a look which she rightly interpreted.

'After dinner?' she prompted, and he brightened visibly.

'I am not a slave-driver? Just a short spell perhaps—not every evening, of course. I am so anxious to get the book finished.'

'Well, of course you are,' agreed Cressida bracingly, 'and I can see no reason why we shouldn't go ahead like wildfire. You have the manuscript here? Have the publishers given you a date?'

The doctor settled back in his chair. 'The manuscript is almost finished—just the final chapter and of course the whole thing to be given a final correction. It's in longhand, I'm afraid, and my writing . . .'

Cressida nodded. Doctors were notoriously bad writers; she had become adept at deciphering their almost unreadable scrawls. 'And the date for the publisher?' she reminded him.

He shuffled the pile of papers before him into thorough disorder until he unearthed a letter. 'Let me see, today is October the twenty-sixth and they ask for the completed typescript by December the twelfth.'

'Is it a long book?' asked Cressida faintly, with visions of getting to bed at three o'clock in the morning and getting up again at six. She was a good typist, but rusty, and she had only two hands—besides, he had hinted himself that his writing was awful.

'Oh, no—eight chapters, about nine thousand words in each, and I believe you will be able to reduce those, for I tend to write with too much elaboration, especially in English.'

'You would like me to check that? But I don't know anything about . . .'

He lifted a podgy hand. 'My dear young lady, I am sure that I can rely on your judgment—it is merely a question of simplifying my English where it is necessary.'

I shall have to take the wretched manuscript to bed, thought Cressida gloomily, and check every word of it. Well, she had wanted something different; it looked as though she had got it, and yet she had the feeling that she had found exactly what she needed; a job which would keep her on her toes and help her to forget the last sad weeks. And when it was finished and she returned to England, perhaps she would be able to settle down to another job in hospital—another ward to run, surgery this time, perhaps. She sighed without knowing it and Doctor van Blom said quickly: 'You are tired—I have no right to expect you to start work so soon after your arrival.'

It took her a minute or two to assure him that she wasn't tired at all and only too willing to start then and there.

They worked together for the rest of the afternoon, and Cressida, glad to have something to occupy her mind, sorted pages, skimmed through the first chapters and then arranged her desk to her satisfaction before typing the first few pages. She had learned to type years ago, before she had trained as a nurse, and she had kept her hand in ever since, typing her father's sermons, the parish magazine and quite a number of his letters when she had been home for holidays or days off; she was pleased and surprised to find that she hadn't lost her skill, and moreover, Doctor van Blom's book was going to be interesting, although she could see that his English was indeed on the elaborate side. She made one or two tentative suggestions which he accepted immediately, saying happily: 'This is just what I needed—someone to check my errors. You will prove yourself to be of the greatest help, Cressida.' He beamed at her. 'You are the answer to a prayer, my dear young lady.'

She hadn't been called anyone's young lady for quite some time, although her father's friends had frequently addressed her as such—elderly gentlemen who had known her since she was a little girl —but now she was very nearly twenty-seven. Doctor van der Teile had called her young woman, which hadn't sounded nice at all—perhaps it was the way he had said it. It was strange that they should have met again and still more strange that he should have made that remark about their meeting being inevitable ... She frowned and her companion said instantly: 'You have difficulty? My writing, perhaps?'

She hastened to reassure him; she mustn't allow her thoughts to wander; a month was hardly time enough to get the book ready for the publisher and certainly didn't allow for any other thoughts than those concerned with it.

The day passed pleasantly; her elderly companions absorbed her into their household with kindly speed, so that she felt at once at ease with them— indeed, they kept her talking so long after dinner that Juffrouw Naald came in, addressed them in severe tones and bore her off to her room, where she pointed to the bed, turned on the bath and produced a glass of hot milk for Cressida to drink—not that she needed any inducement to sleep; her head had no sooner touched the pillow than she was in deep slumber.

It was after breakfast on the third morning, while she was typing out a chapter which Doctor van Blom had decided was now complete, that Doctor van der Teile came in. Cressida, her fingers arrested above the keys, wished him a cool good morning and wondered why she should feel so pleased to see him. After all, he hadn't shown any particular liking for her; indeed, he appeared to dismiss her as a necessary nuisance in his partners' household. Perhaps it was only because she had been wondering about him—his work, where he lived ... She sat with her hands folded quietly in her lap, waiting for him to speak.

'Nose to the grindstone, I see,' he observed without bothering to return her good morning or ask her how she fared. Instead he turned back to open the door for Juffrouw Naald, who steamed in with a coffee tray, set it on the desk, glanced at them in turn with coy speculation, and went away again.

There were two cups on the tray, and: 'You pour,' said Doctor van der Teile.

'I have my coffee at ten o'clock with the doctors, thank you,' Cressida told him a little crossly; he was interrupting her work and disturbing her mind too, and why shouldn't he pour his own coffee?

'It's only nine o'clock, and I missed my breakfast,' and he managed, despite his size and obvious splendid health, to look and sound wistful and half starved. 'Go on,' he urged her, 'be a dear kind girl.' He lifted the lid of the dish on the tray. 'Buttered toast—bless old Naaldtje!'

Cressida picked up the coffee-pot, a handsome silver one of a size made for giants. 'She is extremely kind,' she observed primly.

He took his cup from her, sat down behind his

partner's desk and began on the toast. 'She is also very romantic; she has been trying to find me a suitable wife for the last ten years. She contrives to bring to my notice every likely female she happens to approve of and offer them for my inspection. I rather fancy that you are the latest.'

Cressida choked into her coffee. 'What utter rubbish! I have no intention—it's too silly . . .'

'Well, there's no need to get worked up about it. She means well, bless her, and it isn't as though I've shown any interest in you.'

His voice was bland, and so reasonable that she had to swallow the furious retort she longed to utter, although she did allow herself the comfort of an indignant snort. He took no notice of this but went on: 'In any case, she's wasting her time—I've found the girl for myself and I intend to marry her.'

Cressida nibbled at a biscuit and wondered at the disappointment she was feeling; only a few minutes ago she had wished him married; he needed a wife, for he had by far too big an opinion of himself.

'If she'll have you,' she observed severely.

'Ah, yes. A moot point, although I'm not sure what moot means—we can always deal with that when the time comes.' He passed his cup. 'And how is the book going? Not too much for you, I hope?'

There was silky amusement in his voice and she pinkened. 'The book goes very well, and as I am here merely to type it and make a few small adjustments, I believe that it won't be too much for me.'

'You're a touchy young woman, aren't you? Ready

to swallow me alive, given half a chance.' He passed his cup yet again. 'Any plans to marry?'

Really, the cheek of the man! She said haughtily: 'No.'

The haughtiness went unnoticed or he had a thick skin. 'Boy friend?'

'Certainly not!'

'Ah—I apologise, I shouldn't have asked such a silly question.'

Cressida fired up immediately. 'And why not, pray?'

'Because you are as good as you are beautiful, Cressida.' He smiled at her across the desk, his eyes very bright. 'You are also sad. Why is that?'

She made a great business of putting the cups and saucers back on the tray. The unexpected urge to tell him took her by surprise so that she had to keep a tight hold on her tongue. He didn't even like her, and she was almost sure that she didn't like him, with his easy self-assurance. She shook her head and said nothing at all, and after a moment he said quietly: 'Ah, well, you shall tell me some time —it's good to talk about one's sorrow. It eases it— you must know that from your patients.'

'Yes, oh yes—but listening isn't the same as telling someone ...'

He got up and wandered to the door. 'We all do it at some time,' he pointed out. 'Any messages?'

'Who for?' Her lovely eyes opened in surprise.

'I'm on my way to London, I shall be at the Royal General tomorrow.'

Cressida stared at him; he would ask anyone

33

there and they would tell him why she had left; that her parents had died; that she had had to get away. She said: 'No, thanks,' in a doubtful voice, and he said at once: 'Don't worry, I shan't try to find out anything about you—you'll tell me yourself sooner or later.'

He left her sitting there, staring down at the sheet of typewriting in front of her, the only thought in her head that he would keep his word.

He was back in two days and this time she saw him arrive, for she had been for a brisk walk after lunch, well wrapped up in her good tweed coat against the cold and damp. The sky had been sullen all day and now it was rapidly darkening, the little village looked sombre and bleak and there were already lights in some of the small houses. An afternoon for tea round the fire ... She sighed involuntarily and quickened her step. The book was going very well, but she would have to keep at it. The next day was Sunday and she would be free, but she already had plans to work for a large part of the day. She had nowhere to go and nothing much to do. She would go to church in the morning and then browse through the bookshelves until she found something to her liking. She had her knitting, and any number of letters to write too, but still she felt sure that there would be time and to spare for her typing.

She started round the square towards the doctor's house and then turned her head at the sound of the car coming from the other end—a Bentley, silver grey and sleek, whispering powerfully to a halt. She stood and watched while Doctor van der Teile got out and took the shallow steps two at a time to the front door of her employer's home. Even at that distance she could see that he was elegantly turned out, his car coat making him appear even larger than he was. When the door opened and he had gone inside, she walked on, but instead of using the great brass knocker on the front door, she went past it to the surgery entrance and so to Doctor van Blom's study, where she took off her outdoor things, warmed her chilly hands by the stove and then sat down at her desk. It wasn't time for tea yet, she might as well get another page done.

She had typed just three lines when the door opened and Doctor van der Teile came in. Cressida jumped a little at the suddenness of his appearance and made a muddle of the work she was typing—he was a disquieting person. She erased the mistake, said 'Good afternoon, Doctor,' and gave him an inquiring look.

'Hullo.' He sounded friendly. 'You weren't here just now. Do you use a secret passage or something?'

'I came in through the surgery.'

His eyes rested briefly on her coat. 'Ah—you didn't want to be seen, was that it? Probably you saw me arrive ... All right, you don't have to say anything; your face is an open book. What are you doing tomorrow?'

Really it was no business of his, and yet she found herself giving him a brief resumé of her plans.

'I'll be here at nine o'clock,' he told her. 'Where would you like to go?'

'Go?' repeated Cressida.

'Come, come, girl, you must have some prefer-ence. Leeuwarden? Groningen? the Afsluitdijk? Amsterdam?'

'Are you asking me out?' And before he could reply: 'I was going to church.'

'We will go to Groningen, there is a very beauti-ful church there, then we might go back to Leeu-warden and then Alkmaar.'

She said stiffly: 'You've very kind, but I can't impose on your free time.'

'You won't be; I have to see a friend of mine who lives close to Leeuwarden. He has an English wife who asked me for lunch, and when I told her about you being here she asked me to bring you.' He paused and went on persuasively: 'They have a baby and two toddlers and three dogs.'

Cressida had to laugh. 'Are those an inducement?'

'Yes. I think you like babies and children and dogs. Am I right?'

'How on earth . . .'

'Did I not tell you that your face was easy to read? Will you come?'

'Thank you, I should like to—you're sure your friends won't mind?'

'No, they'll be delighted.' He straightened up from leaning against the door and opened it. 'Shall we have tea?'

'I was going to type . . .'

'After tea.' He waited while she joined him. 'Doc-tor van Blom is delighted with your work; he's a clever man and this book has been his pleasure and study for some time. I fancy it will be well received when it is published.'

Surgery was over for the afternoon and both doctors were back from their rounds. They all had tea together, talking about nothing in particular, and presently Cressida excused herself and went back to her desk. She worked hard until bedtime, spurred on by the thought of her day out on the morrow. She hadn't seen Doctor van der Teile again, although she had heard the Bentley's quiet engine as he drove away later in the afternoon. It struck her that she still had no idea where he lived; it couldn't be far away if he worked in both Leeuwarden and Groningen, and besides, Doctor van Blom had told her that as a general rule he took a surgery with them at least twice a week, but of course he had been in England ...

It would be super to have a day out, seeing something of Holland. She frowned; it would be vexing if they annoyed each other, though. She would have to be careful and frightfully polite whatever he said. After all, he would be giving up quite a lot of his day too, even though they were going to visit his friends. The happy thought that she might be able to glean some information about him from his friend's wife popped into her head as she got into bed and turned out the light. It would be interesting to know—she wasn't being curious, or was she? She fell asleep wondering.

The sky was still sullen when she woke up the next morning and there was more than a hint of rain in the air; she put on a dark green woollen dress she had been saving for some special occasion and brushed her hair into shining smoothness before going down to breakfast. The two doctors were already at table, deeply immersed in some medical argument which Cressida begged them to continue while she drank her coffee and gobbled her roll and cheese. She was putting on her coat when she heard the car draw up in the square below, and pausing just long enough to tug on her round fur hat, snatch up her handbag and gloves and take one last look at herself in the looking glass, she hurried downstairs. At least she hurried until the thought struck her that Doctor van der Teile might be amused to see her rushing to meet him like an enthusiastic schoolgirl. She slowed her impatient feet to a dignified walk, greeted him with pleasant coolness, accepted with a charming smile the two older doctors' good wishes for an enjoyable day, and allowed herself to be ushered out of the house and into the cold morning outside. But the car was warm, deliciously so, with a faint smell of leather. Cressida wrinkled her lovely nose with pleasure at it.

'If you're not warm enough there's a rug in the back,' her companion said laconically as he got in beside her. 'A pity it isn't a better day.'

She murmured something about it being November, feeling suddenly shy; she didn't know this man beside her at all, and on the occasions when they had met they had hardly been on the best of terms. Now the whole day stretched before them. In all likelihood they would fall out within the first hour of it. But long before the hour was up she knew that she had been wrong about that; he had no intention of giving her cause to dislike him, even argue with him. His conversation was confined to the countryside around them until they reached Groningen, and after that they were in St Martin's Church, a splendid edifice about which he seemed to know a great deal. During the service he confined himself to whispered directions as to what came next, finding the hymns for her, and even though she couldn't understand a word of it, opening the prayer book at all the right places.

They lingered on after the service was over, so that she might take a closer look at the dim, lofty interior, and then went outside, where she craned her neck to see the five-storied spire. When she had had her fill, they didn't go back to the car right away, but walked across the vast square and into a wide main street, to drink coffee in one of the cafés there. He was a nice companion, Cressida decided, restful and gently amusing and always ready to answer her questions. The day was going to be fun after all and she started to relax, so that by the time they were in the car once more, speeding towards Leeuwarden, she had lost her shyness and was talking away as though she had known him for years.

The people they were to lunch with lived in a small village west of Leeuwarden and close to Franeker, so that her view of Leeuwarden was confined to a drive round its streets, with the doctor pointing out everything of interest before they drove on, to reach the village, turn in through a great pair of wrought iron gates, and stop finally before a pleasant old house, square and solid and peaceful. But only for a moment; its doors was flung wide and a large, comfortably plump woman stood waiting for them to enter.

'Anna, the housekeeper,' said Doctor van der Teile, and paused on the step while everyone shook hands. 'Ah, here is Harriet.'

His hostess was a year or so older than Cressida, small and dainty and pretty. She came dancing down the staircase to meet them and flung herself at the doctor. He gave her a kiss and a hug and said: 'Harry, this is Cressida, working for Doctor van Blom as I told you.' He left the two girls together and went on into the hall. 'Friso, how's life?'

Friso was large too, and very dark and good-looking. He shook Cressida's hand and exclaimed cheerfully, 'Hullo, how nice to meet you. Giles, this house is filled with women and children— Harry may be only one woman, but she seems like half a dozen—which is delightful, mind you, and the children get into and on to everything.' He smiled at Cressida. 'I hope you like children?'

She said that she did and was borne away to remove her outdoor things and take a quick peep at the baby. 'Ducky, isn't she?' asked Harriet, looking down at her very small daughter in her cot. 'Little Frisco is four and Toby's two and she's almost three months. We're so pleased to have a girl.'

She led the way downstairs again and into the sitting-room, a large, comfortable well-lived-in apartment with easy chairs grouped around a great fire.

The two men were standing before it with the three dogs. J. B., a bulldog, Flotsam, a dog of no known make with an enormous tail and an engaging expression, and a great black shaggy dog with yellow eyes and a great deal of tongue hanging out of its enormous jaws—Moses. They came to meet the two girls, were patted and made much of and rearranged themselves before the fire once more, taking up a lot of room. They all got up again when the door was opened to admit Frisco and Toby, who, having been introduced, got on to their father's knee, where they sat staring at Cressida unwinkingly until it was time to go in to lunch.

It was a delicious meal; onion soup to keep out the cold, as Harriet explained, chicken à la king and a magnificent trifle, which she disclosed with some pride she had made herself. 'It's about all I'm any good at,' she explained to her guests, but Frisco interrupted from his end of the table with: 'You make an excellent stew, my love,' and smiled at her in such a way that a pang smote Cressida's heart. It would be wonderful to be loved like that . . .

'The first meal Harry ever cooked for me was a stew,' Friso told her. 'We ate it in a flooded house under the dyke while the tide came in; it had everything in it and it smelled like heaven.' He put a spoon into Toby's small fist and smiled again at his wife before he went on to talk of something else.

They didn't stay long after lunch, which was a pity because Cressida, robbed of a cosy chat with Harriet, hadn't been able to discover anything about Doctor van der Teile. True, there had been frequent references to mutual friends, but she was still in the dark as to where he lived and what exactly he did. A consultant—well, she knew that, but in which branch of the profession? and had he a practice beside the one he shared—if you could call it sharing—with his partners? And what was his home like and where was it? She wondered if the girl he was going to marry approved of it. She made her farewells with real regret and got into the Bentley.

'Nice people,' commented the doctor as he took the road to the Afsluitdijk and Alkmaar. 'I've known Friso for years, of course—Harry came to Franeker to spend a holiday with a friend and they met there and married in no time.'

They were on the Afsluitdijk now, tearing along its length in the gloom of the afternoon, but Cressida didn't notice the gloom; just for a little while she felt happy and blissfully content; somehow her companion had, in a few hours, lightened her grief. Probably when they next met they would fall out, but for the moment they were enjoying each other's company.

She found Alkmaar enchanting. They parked the car and walked through its narrow streets, looking at the cheese market and the Weigh House, and waiting for the figures on the topmost gable to ride out and encircle the clock when it struck the hour. If it hadn't been so cold, Cressida would have gone back and had another look, but a mean little rain was falling now and the suggestion of tea was welcome. They went to a small tea-room in the main street, almost empty of customers but cosily warm and pretty, with its pink lampshades and small tables. A tiny jug of milk was brought with their miniature teapots, and Cressida, just beginning to get used to the weak, milkless tea the doctors drank, was delighted. Nor did the cake trolley fail in its delights. She chose an elaborate confection of nuts and chocolate and whipped cream and ate it with the gusto of a schoolgirl on a half-term treat, something which caused her companion a good deal of hidden amusement.

It was getting dark as they went into the street again and walked back to the car, and it was as they started back in the direction of Groningen that Cressida inquired artlessly: 'Do you have far to go after you drop me off?'

'No great distance.' And that was all he said, and that in a cool voice which didn't invite any more questions. Probably he thought that she was being curious, but he need not have sounded so snubbing. In a polite, wooden voice she remarked: 'What a pity it is dark so quickly, but I have enjoyed my day—it was so kind . . .'

'It's not over yet, and I'm not kind. I felt like company.'

Her pleasure in the day evaporated and gave way to temper, so that she said tartly: 'How convenient for you that I accepted your invitation, although now that I come to think about it, you didn't invite me—you took it for granted that I'd come.' She added sweetly, 'Pray don't expect that a second time.'

'Who said anything about a second time?' he

wanted to know silkily, and put his foot down hard, so that the Bentley shot forward at a pace to make her catch her breath. Nothing would have made her ask him to drive more slowly, so she sat as still as a mouse and as stiff as a poker until he remarked carelessly: 'It's all right you don't need to be frightened.'

If it had been physically possible, she would have liked to box his ears for him.

They left Afsluitdijk behind them and he slowed the car through Franeker and Leeuwarden and slowed it still more as they neared the village. Cressida, mindful of her manners, had sustained a conversation throughout the latter part of their journey; she would dearly have loved to sulk, but that would have been childish and got her nowhere; dignity was the thing. It made her sit up very straight beside him and talk nothings in a high voice, hurrying from one harmless topic to the next, giving him no time to do more than answer briefly to each well-tried platitude which passed her lips. Dignity, too, helped her to mount the steps to the front door beside him, still talking, to pause at the door and plunge into stilted thanks which he ruthlessly interrupted.

'I'm not coming in,' he told her. 'I had thought that we might have dined together, but at the rate you are going, you would have had no social conversation left, and by the time we had finished the soup you would have been hoarse.'

Cressida's mouth was open to speak her mind, but she didn't get the chance. 'My fault,' he said, and didn't tell her why, and when Juffrouw Naald opened the door he turned without a word and went back to the car. Cressida went indoors feeling as though she had been dropped from a great height and had the breath knocked out of her. It wasn't a nice sensation and she didn't go too deeply into it. She had her supper with the two doctors and went to bed early, expecting to lie awake with her disturbing thoughts, but surprisingly she didn't; she was conscious of only one vivid memory; Doctor van der Teile's lonely back as he had walked away from her on the doorstep.

CHAPTER THREE

THE first thing she thought of when she woke up the next morning was Doctor van der Teile, and the second that he had made no mention of the Royal General, nor asked her a single question about herself. She got up and dressed rapidly, telling herself rather peevishly that quite likely he wasn't in the least interested in her—and why should she mind that? She wasn't interested in him. She scowled horribly at her lovely reflection and went downstairs to thump her typewriter with such speed and energy that Doctor van Blom, when he joined her presently, begged her not to tire herself out so early in the day.

They made good progress during the next few days; the book was taking shape, and Doctor van Blom, now that there was someone to sort out his muddle of notes and reduce his flowery prose to matter-of-fact English, was happier than ever. He worked too hard, of course; he and Doctor Herrima had scant leisure and quite often not enough sleep, and Cressida found herself wondering if their senior partner realised just how busy they were. And he? Most likely leading the well-ordered life of a top consultant, with only urgent cases disturbing his nights; junior doctors to do the spadework for him in hospital and almost certainly a nurse and secretary to help him in his consulting rooms. She worried

46

away about it while it nagged the back of her mind, and when one morning, just as she was putting the finishing touches to a chapter before her coffee break, she heard the Bentley slide to a standstill outside the house, she got to her feet with the half-formed resolve to speak to him about it eddying around her head.

But half way to the door she paused. Mingled with the doctor's deep voice, addressing Juffrouw Naald at the door, was a woman's voice, light and laughing, saying something which made the doctor laugh in his turn. Cressida went back to her desk and put a clean sheet of paper in her machine and began on the next chapter. She would give coffee a miss; she had plenty of work to get on with and it would be a frightful waste of time to go to the sitting-room ... the door opened and Doctor van Blom put his elderly head round it. 'Cressida, coffee is ready—why do you not come?'

'Well, I thought I'd get on with the next chapter —it's going so well ...'

'All the more reason for you to take a little break.' He smiled and held the door wide so that she had no choice but to go with him.

The moment she entered the sitting-room she wished that she hadn't come; the woman sitting by the stove was everything that she had always wanted to be; her pretty face exquisitely made up, a fur coat tossed carelessly over a chair, a velvet trifle arranged just so on her fair hair, the hands she held out to the warmth white and narrow with pink nails. Cressida was all at once conscious of her hastily powdered face, and hair put up with more speed than style, and her tweed skirt, well cut though it was and its matching angora jumper, were no match for the visitor's cashmere two-piece.

She was led to the stove and introduced. 'Monique de Vries,' said Doctor van Blom, 'a great friend of us all and especially of Giles,' and Cressida shook hands and listened to the artless voice speaking in a charmingly broken English, making all the right remarks, smiling across at Doctor van der Teile as she did so as though she shared some delightful secret with him. Perhaps she did, thought Cressida sourly, and good luck to her.

She made suitable replies to the visitor's conversation as she took stock of her; not young, well into her thirties, but so skilfully made up that no one— no man, at least—would know that. She was aware that Doctor van der Teile was watching her, and she looked at him just long enough to wish him good morning. There was a thoughtful look on his face and he didn't smile; he didn't greet her either, only grunted in what she considered to be a very rude manner. She turned a shoulder to him, accepted coffee from Doctor Herrima and embarked on somewhat wishy-washy chat about the weather while she drank it, and then excused herself gracefully and went back to the study.

There would be no chance of talking to Doctor van der Teile now; he obviously had a day off from his work, for his appearance was that of a man of leisure who had nothing much to do, who slept soundly each night without the telephone to drag him awake and who had the time to take his meals at his leisure too—he wouldn't be interested. It was really most unfair.

The door opened and he came in, shutting it behind him. 'What have I done?' he asked mildly.

'Done?'

'Or said—or not done and not said.'

It was a splendid opportunity to speak her mind, but now that she had the chance, she found it surprisingly difficult to start. He sat down in one of the chairs by the stove and looked at her without speaking, so that presently she said in a voice a little louder than usual: 'They're overworked. I've been here just over a week and they're on the go all the time and they're not young any more; out at night, at everyone's beck and call.'

His voice was still mild, dangerously so, she thought. 'And I should do something about it?'

She had the bit nicely between her strong white teeth now. 'Yes—you're still young, and—and probably you have more leisure ...'

'Ah, yes. Naturally.' His face was bland but there was a nasty little smile twisting his mouth. 'A consultant has any amount of time on his hands, underlings to do the chores for him, someone to write his letters; such a life of leisure tends to make him selfish.'

Cressida didn't like the smile at all, nor the glint in his eyes, but she said gamely: 'It's none of my business ...' and was brought to a halt by his silky: 'You're quite right, it is none of your business. If I were you, I should confine myself to the work I

49

am being paid for and try to keep my nose out of other people's affairs.' He got to his feet, looming very large, and strolled to the door. 'I'm glad to hear that you consider me still young,' he observed reflectively.

Cressida thumped her desk with a furious fist. 'You are extremely rude—you could at least treat me with common courtesy!'

He paused to look at her, his head a little on one side. 'No, I don't think I could do that.' He left the room without another word, leaving her to sit and worry. He had been quite insufferable, but she supposed she had deserved it, and he had been quite right; she had no business to poke her nose into other people's lives, she was a stranger in the house and she had only got what she had asked for. All the same, she remembered Doctor Herrima's tired face at breakfast that morning because he had been out most of the night—interfering or not, she was glad that she had spoken as she had. Perhaps Doctor van der Teile would think it over and do something about it.

She typed half a page and then paused to think again. There had been a receptionist before she came—an older woman who had retired and left the village, and no one had come to replace her. It was difficult, Doctor van Blom had explained, to get a young woman to take a job in the country, and the hours were awkward. Cressida typed the rest of the page and before she started on the next one, paused to think again. The book was taking all her time, but when it was done, perhaps she could stay on.

She would have to learn to speak and understand Dutch pretty quickly, but surely to begin with she could get by with the basics of that language? The idea was worth thinking about later on. She began to type again and kept on steadily until it was time for lunch.

There was a letter from her aunt in the morning, enclosing a newspaper cutting; there was a 'flu epidemic imminent in the western world, it stated, a virulent type, too, equally bad for young and old. Aunt Emily added a postscript of her own, telling her to take care of herself. Cressida showed it to Doctor Blom later in the morning and he startled her by nodding agreement with it. 'This is quite true, there are already a number of cases—Giles warned us.'

She had a vivid little picture of him, sitting at an imposing desk, telling his secretary to be sure to warn his partners. 'I wonder what he specialises in?' she said out aloud.

Her companion answered her with ready enthusiasm. 'Chests. Bronchial conditions, asthma, C A of lung, emphysema ... he's one of the best men we've got at the moment. Brilliant, quite brilliant; never spares himself, either.'

Cressida couldn't agree with this; Doctor van der Teile had been sparing himself on the previous day, and in good company too. She asked quickly before she could think better of doing so, 'Mevrouw de Vries—you said she was a great friend.'

Doctor van Blom cast a lightning glance over the tops of his old-fashioned gold-rimmed spectacles.

'And so she is—her late husband was Giles' best friend. A charming lady, is she not?' He smiled guilelessly. 'She amuses him, for she is always lively. They have known each other for many years.'

'She looks so young,' observed Cressida innocently, and felt mean because he said at once, 'She is a very pretty woman still, but she must be nearing forty. Her husband—Wim—died, let me see, it must be four years ago. He left her comfortably off and they had no children, so she is able to live as she likes.' He gave her another look. 'You are interested in her, Cressida?'

She had been on the point of asking where the lady lived, and then, given the chance, leading the conversation round to Doctor van der Teile to find out where he lived, too, but she saw that that wouldn't do. She said instead: 'People are always interested in pretty women, you know. Would you like to read this paragraph before you go? I've turned some of it round the other way, but I'd like you to approve it before I get it typed.'

'Of course. We really are getting on with the book now, aren't we? I seemed in such a muddle before you came, but now you have tidied it all up so nicely.'

'Well, it's so much easier for a strange eye. With luck it will be ready before the publisher has asked for it.' They exchanged the pleased smiles of two people who had worked hard and were reaping their reward, before they settled down to work again.

There was a case of 'flu the next morning—an elderly man in one of the outlying farms; he had been poorly for several days, but he had been tough all his life; there was no need to call the doctor, he had told his wife, and by the time she had made up her mind to disobey him, it was too late—he died very shortly after Doctor van Blom got to him. There were two more cases the next day, and then two more, and on the third day it was in the village itself. Cressida, who relied on her skeleton news each morning from whichever doctor had the time or inclination to translate it for her, asked anxiously if the epidemic was spreading.

'I fear so,' said Doctor van Blom, 'and all over Europe. It is bad in England, especially in the eastern counties, and it is most serious in Germany and France, also Belgium, and here in Holland it is bad too. The hospitals are already full. We are asked whenever possible to treat the patients at home unless life is in danger. Fortunately, if we can get at it in its early stages, antibiotics will help, although it is a pity that this particular virus has not yet been identified. You are not nervous, Cressida?'

'Me? Heavens, no. I was wondering if I might help a little. I could cut down on the book for a few days and give you a hand in the surgery. I know I shan't be of much use because I can't speak Dutch, but I can understand just a little, and I could give injections, and take blood pressures and put on bandages, things like that. It might give you more time for the important cases.'

She looked at her elderly companions; they were both tired, she thought worriedly, and no wonder. They had had no time to themselves for several days

53

now and there had been no sign of Doctor van der Teile. Surely he was supposed to take the surgery twice a week? She was on the point of mentioning this when Doctor Herrima coughed and said in his nice, slow voice, 'That is very kind of you, Cressida. I think we shall be very pleased to accept your offer. As you suggest, there are a great many small tasks which you might undertake, and just at present we are busy.'

'Good. I'll start right away, shall I? I suppose there isn't an overall I could borrow?'

The garment was found and Juffrouw Naald pinned her into it, and rather nervous now that the actual moment had arrived to start work, Cressida went into the waiting room.

It was packed out with a cross-section from the village inhabitants and the neighbouring hamlets and farms; small boys with arm plasters, crying babies, elderly gentlemen with thunderous coughs, small, sniffing, tearful children and their mothers. Just one with 'flu, thought Cressida gloomily, and everyone will get it. But she didn't allow the gloom to show. She smiled at them all, wished them good day in her bad Dutch and went to tap on Doctor Herrima's door.

'Could you let me have a list of patients?' she asked him. 'I'll send them in and that will save you getting out of your chair each time. Is there a bell?'

There was. One ring for the next patient, two rings if she was wanted. She crossed the room to Doctor van Blom's door and repeated the exercise and then, armed with her lists, went back to the waiting room and called the first name, 'Juffrouw Aapinga', who proved to be a very old lady indeed who needed help to walk to Doctor Herrima's surgery before she was free to inquire from the faces round her which of them was Aerde Welmer. He turned out to be a small boy with an arm plaster and a scowl, accompanied by an elder sister. Cressida ushered the pair of them into Doctor van Blom's surgery and went back to the old lady; Doctor Herrima would want her coat off ...

They were drinking their coffee two hours later when Cressida asked: 'Where do they all come from? I mean, the surgery was packed, and such a variety of complaints.'

'The time of year—and probably this afternoon there will be no one at all.'

He was wrong, of course. True, there were only five patients in the waiting room when Cressida went in. Two of them wanted their ears syringed, the other three had 'flu.

The next day the surgery was almost empty, but the telephone rang all round the clock. Juffrouw Naald, a tower of strength in any emergency, provided hot food at all hours and appeared with piping hot coffee just when it was most needed, and for the unfortunate who was called out during the night, there was a thermos jug of hot chocolate standing on the hall table. Cressida, although she didn't need to get up at night, lay awake in her pleasant room, listening to the doctors' quiet footfall and the tinkle of the telephone, and after two such nights, she suggested to her tired companions at breakfast that perhaps it might be a good idea if she were to forsake her typing altogether for the moment and give a hand in some other way. 'I could drive you on your rounds,' she suggested diffidently, 'then you could at least rest between visits. I'm quite a good driver and I've got my licence with me.'

'My Chevrolet?' asked Doctor Blom doubtfully. 'Is that not too powerful a car for a girl to drive, my dear?'

'Well, no, I don't think so. Could I not try it? And if you don't like the idea I won't go on with it.' She studied their middle-aged faces. What they both needed was a night's uninterrupted sleep. Surely Doctor van der Teile could take over for a couple of nights so that his partners could have a much-needed rest? It was unlikely that he would go out much at night and she could see no reason why he shouldn't take his share in the circumstances. If she had known his telephone number, or even where he lived or worked, she would have got up from the table then and there and telephoned him, whether it was her business or not, but she didn't know, and when she suggested tactfully that they should get in touch with him and ask him to lend a hand, she was gently but firmly discouraged from continuing the conversation.

Her days were full now; despite her lack of Dutch, she managed in the surgery well enough, and after an initial nervousness, she managed the Chev and Doctor Herrima's BMW as well, so that once they had allayed their fears about her inability to drive, they were able to sit beside her, relaxing or even, at times, dropping off into a light doze.

She was driving Doctor van Blom back from his afternoon calls when she happened to glance at him and saw how ill he looked. Her heart sank; it wasn't exhaustion which made him look so ghastly, she had seen enough 'flu victims by now to know that, and not only did he look awful; his breathing was laboured and his eyes were closed. She broke his rigid rule about the Chev's speed and sent the needle up between ninety and a hundred and prayed that Doctor Herrima would be home.

He was; they got Doctor van Blom up to his bed and into it, and he raised no objection at all, but lay very quiet, not even bothering to open his eyes, and when Doctor Herrima plunged the antibiotic into him he didn't seem to notice that either. Doctor Herrima was called out a few minutes later, leaving Cressida to look after his partner, and Juffrouw Naald to answer the door bell and the telephone and provide, as it were, a supporting line.

It was some two hours later that the housekeeper came silently into the room to tell Cressida, in one-syllable Dutch and a good deal of sign language, that Doctor Herrima was delayed; might not even be back until midnight or later—a baby, said Juffrouw Naald.

Cressida went to look at her patient again; his pulse was rising, so was his temperature, and his breathing was getting more difficult, but Doctor Herrima had left instructions that the next dose of antibiotic wasn't to be given before midnight. It seemed to her that that particular antibiotic wasn't

57

doing its work—something else should be tried without delay. Juffrouw Naald had gone downstairs again, leaving her a heartening cup of coffee, and now she took the cup in her hand and prowled round the room. She was looking for Doctor van Blom's little notebook in which he kept telephone numbers; she had seen it a dozen times, for he had a habit of leaving it around in the oddest places. It had struck her suddenly that possibly Doctor van der Teile's number would be in it. If she could find the book and it was, she was going to telephone him.

She found the book under a chair, and his number was in it, or at least, there were three numbers, two in Groningen and one in Leeuwarden. She dialled the first number and a man's voice answered and she asked to speak to the doctor urgently. The voice told her to hold the line in quite tolerable English, and after a few minutes which seemed like hours to her, she heard the doctor's 'Hullo, Cressida.' He sounded in a hurry and there was a faint question in his voice.

She didn't waste time but plunged at once: 'Doctor van Blom has 'flu and he's ill. He's in bed and Doctor Herrima gave him a shot of antibiotic more than two hours ago, but he's not responding and Doctor Herrima is out on a baby case and doesn't expect to be back until midnight at the earliest. You've got to do something . . .' She had started off calmly, but now, to her vexation, she heard her voice spiralling higher and higher.

The doctor heard it too. 'Don't panic,' his voice was quiet in her ear. 'I can't come immediately, but I'll be with you in, let me see ...' he paused, presumably to look at his watch, and she heard him speak to someone and a woman's voice reply. 'An hour, perhaps—it may be longer. Keep a sharp eye on him.' He rang off without saying goodbye.

It was almost two hours before her anxious ears heard the Bentley coming round the square. Doctor Herrima was still out and Juffrouw Naald, who had refused to go to bed, had appeared silently with coffee and a reassuring air which had changed to satisfaction when Cressida had told her what she had done. She listened now to the opening of the house door and the murmur of voices, and a moment later Doctor van der Teile was in the room, dwarfing everything there with his size. He nodded at her without speaking and went to bend over his partner. Presently he straightened up and said across the bed: 'Tell me about it.'

She told him, in a concise, unhurried manner, not forgetting anything and not exaggerating either, and when she had finished he opened his bag and took out a syringe and phial. 'I'm going to try this —we've been having some success with it—it must be repeated in three hours, and keep on with the hourly T.P.R. Get him to drink if you can, if not I'll have to get a drip up.'

Cressida moved round beside him to hold a lamp so that he could see what he was doing, and for the first time in the dimly lit room, saw his face clearly. 'My goodness, you're tired!' she jerked out in surprise, seeing the deep lines etched between nose and mouth and his weary eyes.

He flicked her a mocking glance. 'You see what a life of ease and idleness does to a man,' he observed blandly. 'Where's Doctor Herrima?'

'At Tjalkes Farm—Mevrouw Tjalkes went into labour late this afternoon—it's a first baby. Doctor Herrima thought it would be a long case.'

'It's close on midnight. Were there any other urgent calls?'

She was arranging the bedclothes carefully. 'Yes, two. Old Mevrouw Jagersma across the square complaining of her chest, and Mijnheer Kulk with a pain in his leg.'

'Your Dutch has improved enormously since I last saw you.' He was laughing at her, but she answered seriously,

'No. Juffrouw Naald takes the messages and we manage to understand each other very well. I asked her to tell them that there wasn't a doctor available but he'd come as soon as he could.'

He nodded. 'Stay here, I'll be back.' He had gone. Cressida heard his almost silent step on the stair, Juffrouw Naald's fierce whisper, the clink of cup on saucer and then the closing of the front door. His steps sounded louder in the square outside as he walked the few yards to Mevrouw Jagersma's little house.

He was back quite soon, beside her, looking over her shoulder at her neatly kept chart.

'Mevrouw Jagersma?' she asked in a whisper.

'A mild coronary. There'll be an ambulance very soon—her daughter's with her. I'm going to Mijnheer Kulk and then on to the Tjalkes'.'

He had gone again, leaving the room full of vitality and confidence.

Cressida managed to keep awake somehow, walking about the room in her stockinged feet, drinking cup after cup of strong coffee. She had persuaded Juffrouw Naald to go to bed and made her understand that she would be of far more use in the morning, when everyone else would be dead on their feet. The house was quiet save for the doctor's troubled breathing, and that, she fancied, was a trifle easier; his pulse was slower too. She gave him his second injection on time, and resumed her prowling. The ambulance had come and gone again, the square outside was pitch dark and still. She shivered with tiredness and the cold that comes from lack of sleep, and then went back to the window; a long way off still she could hear a car engine—two, and a few seconds later she could see their lights across the flat country. Juffrouw Naald had left coffee on the stove in the kitchen and a tray of sandwiches besides. Cressida looked at her sleeping patient and decided that the men could help themselves; she would stay where she was until they had taken a look at their partner.

The cars stopped with only a whisper of sound before the house, and she had to strain her ears to hear the doctors come in. They entered the room together and went straight to the bed, to bend over it and mutter together. Presently Doctor van der Tcile straightened himself and came over to where she was standing. 'He's no worse,' he told her. 'You'll have seen that for yourself.' He looked down at

61

her weary face. 'Is Naaldtje in bed?'

'Yes, about two hours ago, although she didn't want to go.'

'Unnatural woman! And you? You look as though you could do with some sleep.'

'Doctor van Blom can't be left. I'll go to bed when Juffrouw Naald is up and about again.'

'You'll go now, Cressida. We shall want you wide awake enough to drive one or other of us on our rounds later. We'll manage morning surgery between us.'

She eyed Doctor Herrima across the room and Doctor van der Teile said quietly, 'He's going to bed now.'

'What about you?' she wanted to know, and regretted the question the moment she had uttered it, for he smiled quite nastily.

'Should I be flattered by your concern? Surely I'm only getting what I deserve?'

He had strolled away to speak to his partner before she could think of a reply to that, and when the older man told her kindly to go to bed, she went without another word.

She was awakened by Joukje, the young girl who came in to help Juffrouw Naald, bearing a tray with coffee and rolls, and Cressida, rubbing the sleep from her eyes, saw with horror that it was almost ten o'clock. It was of no use engaging the girl in conversation, so she took the tray with a smile of thanks and the moment Joukje had gone, jumped out of bed. She bathed and dressed in slacks and a sweater, breakfasting as she did so, feeling horribly guilty, and then went along to see how Doctor van Blom was. He was asleep, so she lost no time in going downstairs where she found the doctors having their coffee, making up their morning rounds. Doctor Herrima looked every day of his sixty years despite his brief sleep, but Doctor van der Teile, with his back to the dull morning light, appeared at first glance to be his usual immaculate self. Only as Cressida crossed the room did she see that the lines were still there and a little deeper, and his eyes were heavy-lidded although alert still.

They had both got to their feet as she went in, although she begged them not to. Doctor Herrima sank back into his chair, but his younger partner stayed on his feet, saying in a matter-of-fact voice: 'Hullo—we've been planning the work load. Doctor Herrima is going to bed now—luckily there is no afternoon surgery. Naaldtje will keep an eye on Doctor van Blom, who is holding his own quite nicely, and you are to drive me on the morning round. With luck we should get an hour's rest before the afternoon visits. Doctor Herrima will take the evening surgery while you and I take to our beds—I'll take any night calls and can keep a watchful eye on Doctor van Blom for the second half of the night. It's a poor plan at its best, but it will have to do. There's no help to be got—nurses and doctors are in short supply and we must manage as best we can.'

Cressida considered carefully and then remarked kindly: 'I think that's quite well arranged. I can see one or two holes in it, but I expect you saw them too and there's nothing much to be done about them. is there? I'm sure we can manage. Is there anything you want me to do for Doctor van Blom before we go?'

Doctor Herrima had nodded off. 'No. Naaldtje and I dealt with the necessities. If you are ready shall we get started?'

She went back upstairs and got into her coat and a warm headscarf; it was raw outside and she still felt cold. She wondered which car she was to drive, and when she got downstairs she discovered that it was to be the Bentley.

She paused at the front door to say: 'Do you mean to say that you trust me to drive your car?'

He glanced down at her and then back at the gloves he was putting on. 'My dear girl, what has that to do with it? I badly need to sleep, even if in short snatches, and I can see no other way of doing it.'

'Well!' said Cressida on an indignant breath, and swept down the steps. Indignation got her into the driving seat and stiffened her spine so that she drove off with something of a flourish and quite forgot to be nervous because she was driving a Bentley.

'The Tjalkes first. Across the square and follow the road on the left for five kilometres. There's a turning on the right, and you can see the farm from the road. Wake me up when we're there.'

She cast him an indignant glance and saw that his eyes were already shut.

They were back by one o'clock and they could

have got back sooner than that, but she had taken pity on him and slowed down between the less urgent cases so that he might doze for a few precious minutes.

She hadn't expected to feel hungry, but Juffrouw Naald was waiting for them with a tureen of *erwten* soup, hot and savoury and satisfying. She ate with appetite and went upstairs to attend to Doctor van Blom's small wants. He was feeling a little better and being, on the whole, a good patient, although his chest was proving troublesome. She gave him an inhalation, tucked him up again for the afternoon with strict instructions to drink all the lemonade she had put on his bedside table, and went to her own room. It was too late to have a rest; the afternoon rounds were almost due, so she did her face again and her hair, changed her sweater and slacks for a jersey dress, put on her coat once more and went downstairs to the hall. Doctor van der Teile was already there, sitting in a leather armchair in one corner, fast asleep. She stood for a moment looking at him while she admitted that he was proving a tower of strength, although she couldn't understand why he had waited until she had telephoned before coming to his partners' aid. He must have known that they were hard pressed, and besides, even then, he hadn't come at once and he had sounded annoyed—no, not annoyed, but there had been something ... She stretched out a hand and touched him gently. 'Doctor van der Teile, should we be going?' Her voice was as gentle as her touch.

His eyes opened immediately, their gaze clear and

steady, and although he didn't speak Cressida found herself flushing under his look and when he smiled she looked away; she hadn't seen him smile like that before, it made her heart jump in a ridiculous fashion and upset her breathing. She must have been more tired than she realised, she told herself, and asked briskly which patient he intended visiting first.

The round was finished more quickly than that of the morning; this time she didn't slow down the Bentley's pace at all, but spurred on by the prospect of bed, she drove fast. It meant that her companion had very little time to doze, but he would be in his bed all the sooner.

There was a meal waiting for them when they got in, but she went first of all to see how Doctor van Blom was faring, and Doctor van der Teile went with her. Only when he was quite satisfied as to his colleague's condition did he go away again, leaving her to freshen up the bed, get her patient a drink and take his temperature, and by the time she had done this she was too tired to go downstairs again.

She undressed in a haphazard way, let her hair fall from its pins, got into her nightdress and climbed into bed. Her lovely, untidy head had barely touched the pillow when there was a knock on the door and Doctor van der Teile came in carrying a tray upon which reposed a cup and saucer and a steaming bowl. 'I advise you to have this,' he observed in a kindly impersonal doctor's voice, 'or you will be awake in a couple of hours, dying of hunger.'

He gave her the tray and sat down in a chair by the window. 'And do hurry up,' he begged her, 'otherwise I shall go to sleep too, and that would never do.'

She was too tired to say anything, although she knew that he was right. She ate the soup in the bowl and then drank her tea, her eyes owl-like in her pale face. When she had finished he took the tray from her and tucked her up as though she had been a little girl. She was almost asleep by then, so that it might have been the edge of a dream when she felt his kiss on her cheek.

CHAPTER FOUR

JUFFROUW NAALD, bearing a tray of tea and sandwiches, wakened Cressida before midnight, her tall spare frame wrapped cosily in a woolly dressing gown of a thickness to defy the coldest night. She set the tray down, nodded and smiled and pointed to the clock, patted Cressida on the shoulder and said *'Arme kind,'* and Cressida smiled sleepily back. It was comforting to be called a poor child in that motherly voice—indeed, she wished very much that she could cast herself upon the dear soul and have a good weep. Instead she sat up in bed with what she hoped was alert wakefulness while the housekeeper conveyed the news that Doctor van Blom was holding his own still, that there were three more cases of 'flu in the village, and that she herself was about to retire for the night. She then wished Cressida a good night and departed, whereupon Cressida tossed back the bedclothes and between bites and gulps contrived to shower, get into slacks and sweater, tie her hair back without much regard to style, and with no make-up on her pretty, still sleepy face, made her way to her patient's room.

He was awake and greeted her with a weak smile, unlike Doctor van der Teile, standing by the bed, who had frowned across the room at her as though she was the very last person he wanted to see.

'Oh,' said Cressida, taken aback by the fierceness of the frown, 'I didn't know ... I just popped along to see ... I'll come back.' She smiled at Doctor van Blom, cast a cold look at his partner, who was still frowning, and slid away to the kitchen.

She was setting the place to rights when he joined her. He was wearing slacks and a vast sweater and somehow managed to look wide awake, well rested and faultlessly turned out at the same time. He wasted no time on pleasantries. 'I'm not too happy about Doctor van Blom's chest,' he observed, and from his manner he might have been in the middle of a consultant's round with a bevy of students, nurses, physiotherapists and the like, hanging upon his every word. 'I should like him well sat up throughout the night, inhalations three-hourly, pulse hourly, and he must be encouraged to cough. He must also drink all the fluids you can get into him. His antibiotic is due in two hours' time and again at six o'clock. He has refused his sleeping tablets. Doctor Herrima is in bed; he'll take morning surgery and the morning visits. Naaldtje will be down at seven o'clock. Have your breakfast before then if you can and then go to bed; I shall need you to help with the afternoon surgery and the visits afterwards.'

She listened to this string of instructions, said 'O.K.,' rather pertly and asked: 'And you? What are you going to do?'

She watched his eyebrows climb in surprise. 'Is it necessary for you to know? I'm not in the habit ...'

'Oh, stuff,' said Cressida roundly, 'you're not in

69

your consulting rooms now, you know. Supposing I should want you in a hurry, where will you be? Bed?'

His smile was nasty, but she deserved it, she supposed. 'You're a cheeky young woman. I shall be in the surgery writing up notes and filling in forms. Should I have to go out I will either let you know or leave a note by the telephone.'

He had gone before she could answer him.

She heard the telephone shortly after she had gone back upstairs to settle Doctor van Blom down for a nap, and very soon after that the Bentley's gentle purr, and when her patient slept she padded downstairs to have a look by the telephone. Sure enough, there was a message. He had been called out to Wolkertsje Willemse, a five-year-old girl Cressida had seen in the surgery not many days since. He had added the telephone number, and as she was reading it, the telephone rang. She answered it in some trepidation; she had had to take messages once or twice already and hadn't enjoyed it at all, but this time it was a young farmer whose wife had been at the surgery only the day before and who was expecting a baby in a few weeks' time. Cressida warned him in her careful Dutch: 'Speak slowly,' and then listened carefully to his excited voice: the baby—several weeks early, and could the doctor go at once?

Cressida reassured him in her peculiar mixture of English and Dutch, heavily interlarded with O.K.s, remembered to take his telephone number and then dialled the Willemses' house. She had to wait for the doctor and when he did get to the telephone, all he said in a terse voice was: 'Well?'

She explained. 'And here's the number. I don't know how long she's been in labour. Is there anything I can do?'

'No. This child's ill, she'll have to go to hospital. I'll telephone about the baby and go there as soon as the ambulance gets here. Are you managing?'

She said yes, stoutly. 'And if I can't understand, I'll give them the number where you're most likely to be.'

There were two more calls after that, both, as far as she could understand, urgent. She tracked down the doctor and passed on the names and addresses and what she hoped was the right information and went back to Doctor van Blom, who dozed and woke and became fretful towards morning. But his temperature was down and it seemed to her that his breathing was a good deal easier. There was no sign of Doctor van der Teile by five o'clock; she washed and tidied her restless patient, gave him a cup of tea and had the satisfaction of seeing him sink at last into a refreshing sleep. She was in the kitchen, cutting slices off the loaf while the kettle boiled, when she heard the front door click shut, and Doctor van der Teile came in. He looked dog-tired now, his face drawn and haggard—moreover, he was in need of a shave. He put down his bag on the kitchen table and asked without preamble, 'Doctor van Blom?'

'He seems better, his respirations are down, so is his temperature. He's slept for short periods and since I settled him an hour ago, he's sleeping peacefully.'

She made the tea and put the bread in the toaster, then got another cup and saucer and plate from the dresser. 'You've had a busy night.'

She thought he was going to laugh, but all he said was: 'So-so. Is there any marmalade?'

She fetched the Dundee marmalade the doctors liked with their breakfast and poured the tea. 'Was the baby all right?'

He nodded. 'A boy—he'll do. They're a sensible couple and her mother's on the way there—there isn't a nurse to be had.'

She took the toast from the toaster and put in two more slices. 'Is the epidemic at its height?'

'Just about. It's been hectic ...' She waited to hear what he was about to say, but he changed his mind and passed his cup for more tea. 'You feel able to manage the day's work ahead?'

'Yes, thanks. I'm used to long hours,' she paused, 'or at least I was until I left hospital.'

He buttered toast and piled on the marmalade. Without looking at her: 'Why?'

At any other time she might have declined to answer him, but she was bone-weary, and in that half world of tiredness nothing seemed quite real. 'My father was ill. He died, and my mother died a few days after him.'

Strangely she felt better now she had told him, but it wouldn't do to bore him with details, so she asked him in a bright voice if he would like some more toast.

He was staring at her across the table. 'No doubt you will be furious with yourself for telling me,' his voice was kind and gentle, 'but don't be that— I'm a doctor, you know, and one can tell doctors things one would never dream of mentioning to anyone else. And it's not right to lock one's grief away as though it were something to be ashamed of. Sorrow is for sharing, and so is love. And it has nothing to do with whether we like each other or not; you told your confidence to a doctor, not to a man you aren't quite sure you like.' He grinned tiredly. 'You are at perfect liberty to go on disliking me if you wish, and you may disagree with me as much as you like.'

'I've never said . . .'

'Er—no, not in so many word, but I am a lazy, thoughtless man who has to be reminded of his duty to his partners and has far too easy a life; rich patients filling the consulting rooms, eight hours' sleep every night, leisure to spend the day driving my girl-friends round the country . . .'

'I never . . .' began Cressida once more, bristling with indignation even while she had to admit that was exactly what she had thought of him—but not any more. She looked him in the eye and said soberly: 'You're quite right, I did think something like that, but I don't now; you've been super, working round the clock and never complaining. I daresay it only needed someone to remind you . . .'

He let out a tired roar of laughter and she asked snappily: 'Now what have I said?'

'Oh, my dear girl, you're a dozen women rolled

into one! Go to bed, do, before I say something I shouldn't.'

She had got to her feet, but now she paused. 'What?'

'Never mind what—disregard anything I've said, I'm tired. Disregard this too.' He had come round the table and caught her close. Even with a bristly chin his kiss was something to remember.

After six hours' sleep Cressida felt marvellous; she consumed the meal Juffrouw Naald had brought to her room, then dressed in a skirt and jumper and put her hair up, for if she was to help in the surgery she would have to look tidy. As she dressed she was aware that she would have liked to pause and think over her conversation with Doctor van der Teile. For someone she wasn't quite sure she liked, he was beginning to make quite an impression on her. But there was really no time now. She skipped along to see her patient and found him propped up in bed, the shadow of his former chubby self but feeling decidedly better. She spent a little time with him, washing his hands and face, making his bed and brushing his fringe of hair before taking his temperature and pulse. They were both returning to normal and she saw with satisfaction that his breathing was greatly improved. She stood over him while he drank the glass of lemonade and ate the milk pudding she had fetched for him and then went downstairs, taking the tray with her. Juffrouw Naald was in the kitchen, putting the finishing touches to the nourishing stew she was preparing for their evening meal. She had wisely given up the more elaborate dishes she took such pride in serving, and now produced food which could be eaten quickly and whenever anyone wanted it. She set the saucepan on the stove and smiled at Cressida, looking at the clock. There was almost ten minutes before the afternoon surgery was due to start; without a word she reached for a teapot and made tea, and Cressida, sitting down at the kitchen table to drink it, exclaimed: 'What a dear you are!' and the housekeeper smiled again, understanding what her words implied.

The hot tea topped up her returning energy very nicely. Cressida hurried down the passage and into the hall, ready for work once more. She was half way to the surgery door when the front door was opened and Doctor van der Teile walked in. He was still in his sweater and slacks and a car coat, and although he had shaved, he looked even more tired than he had done at five o'clock that morning.

'You've not been to bed,' she accused him, 'you can't possibly take surgery—what you need is ten hours' sleep . . .' Her voice sharpened. 'Where have you been? Surely not another case?'

He blinked at her as he took off his coat and handed her his bag. 'Put that in the surgery for me, will you? I'll be with you in ten minutes.' He paused at the foot of the staircase. 'No case, Miss Busybody; I had a date with a lady. I couldn't disappoint her even though I knew I ran the risk of being met at the door by a harridan firing questions at me like bullets from a gun.'

He went upstairs two at a time, leaving her gaping open-mouthed after him.

He reappeared in exactly nine minutes, to sit behind Doctor van Blom's desk in his surgery. He was wearing a suit now, a beautifully cut one, Cressida noted as she ushered in the first patient. She liked his tie too; he looked just what he was, a successful consultant, self-assured, impersonal, kind ... and desperately weary. She wondered uneasily if he had had any sleep at all.

Two hours later, driving the Bentley once more through the grey afternoon, she was sure he hadn't, for almost before they had left the house he was asleep. The first visit was some kilometres away so that he had ten minutes before, reluctantly, she woke him up. He slept on and off between each patient and she marvelled how he was able to be instantly alert as she drew up at each house. The list was finished at last and she drove quickly back to the house; they had hardly spoken to each other in the surgery or on the round, and that was hardly to be wondered at, she supposed. Harridan indeed ...! she ground the gears as they rounded the square and sensed him wincing.

In the hall she said coldly, 'It's none of my business, but I think that you should go to bed, Doctor van der Teile!'

'For once we can agree about something, Cressida. Doctor Herrima will take the evening surgery and be on call until midnight. I suggest that you give him a hand and then get to bed yourself. Could you find time to see to Doctor van Blom first?'

He had spoken quite pleasantly; now he turned away and went towards the kitchen, leaving her to go upstairs and start on the task of getting her patient comfortable and ready for the light supper he was allowed.

The evening surgery wasn't too crowded and there were no calls. Cressida and Doctor Herrima ate their meal in peace before she went upstairs again to persuade Doctor van Blom to settle down for the night. To her surprise he needed little persuasion and within half an hour she was able to leave him with a promise of a further visit before she went to bed herself. There had been no further telephone calls, so she went along to the sitting-room to spend half an hour with Doctor Herrima. She found him sitting in his chair and one brief glance at his face told her that here was the next victim of the 'flu. She didn't waste time brooding over the complications his illness would cause to the household. 'You're going to bed,' she told him firmly. 'I'm going to help you this very minute. There aren't any calls and surgery is finished—if anything turns up I'll warn Doctor van der Teile. Besides, Juffrouw Naald is here, and she's a wonderful help.'

He didn't need much persuasion. She could see that he felt ill; past caring about anything much. She helped him upstairs, left him to get into bed and ran downstairs to get a tray of lemonade and a hot drink. She would have to get Doctor van der Teile out of his bed shortly, so that he could write up the antibiotic and confirm that it really was 'flu.

She glanced at the clock. It was four hours since Doctor van der Teile had gone to bed; he hadn't had nearly enough sleep, but there was nothing else she could do. The kitchen door stood open, so she went in, sorting out her small store of Dutch words in order to acquaint Juffrouw Naald of this latest disaster, and then forgot all about them. The house-keeper was sitting at the table, her head in her hands, her eyes closed. She was a nasty colour too, Cressida noted that with a professional eye while she swallowed despair. Somehow she would have to get her up the stairs and into her bed.

Juffrouw Naald opened her eyes and looked at her blankly, muttered something in Dutch and closed them again.

'Bed,' said Cressida brightly, thankful that the word was the same in both languages, and heaved on the housekeeper's arm. Juffrouw Naald was game; somehow she struggled to her feet and tottered out of the kitchen, leaning heavily on Cressida's arm. The pair of them wove their way across the hall like a couple of inebriates and began their difficult climb up the stairs. Cressida, feeling her companion's weight becoming heavier and heavier, despaired of ever reaching the top, but they did, to sink down helplessly on the top step. They would have to get up again, she knew, but for the moment, rest was essential.

Doctor van der Teile's quiet: 'Good God, what in heaven's name are you doing there?' roused her. He was standing outside his room, clad in a magnificent dressing gown, and she said apologetically:

'Did we wake you? I'm so sorry, we tried to be quiet. Juffrouw Naald has the 'flu—I'm just getting her to bed.'

'But she's twice your size.' He had come over to look at the housekeeper she was supporting. 'You silly girl, why didn't you get Doctor Herrima to help you?' He frowned. 'He's still up?'

'No, he's not.' Her voice was tart; silly girl, indeed!—'He's got the 'flu as well.'

The arm he had flung round her shoulders tightened. 'My dear valiant Miss Bingley, why didn't you wake me?' He bent to move the housekeeper to one side and Cressida felt herself whisked to her feet. She stood for a moment, his arm still solidly comfortable round her shoulders. She looked at him and away again. 'You called me a harridan,' she said, as though that explained everything. She felt his arm grip her and then fall away. 'I'll go and turn down her bed.'

She had the covers off by the time he reached the room, carrying Juffrouw Naald. 'Get her to bed, will you?' he asked her. 'I'll go along to Doctor Herrima.'

'Temperature a hundred and three, pulse a hundred and twenty, breathing rapid but not laboured. He's been in bed less than half an hour. I was getting him a drink when I found Juffrouw Naald.'

The doctor nodded. 'I'll take a look at his chest and give him a shot. By that time you'll be ready.'

The housekeeper wasn't all that easy to undress, although she tried very hard to help, but at length she was in bed, sitting up nicely against her pillows.

Doctor van der Teile, when he returned, examined her carefully, gave her an injection too, pronounced himself satisfied that she wasn't too bad, urged her not to worry about anything and went away to dress, leaving Cressida to settle her new patients with drinks and any small comforts they might require. She was coming out of Doctor Herrima's room, having settled them both to her satisfaction, when she met Doctor van der Teile, dressed now and very wide awake.

'Doctor van Blom's asleep, Are there any calls?'

'No, none at all.'

'Good. We'll have some coffee and work out some sort of routine to cover the next twenty-four hours.'

It wasn't easy. Whichever way they looked at it, they were going to be hopelessly short-handed. 'I'll get Joukje to sleep in,' the doctor decided. 'She can get the meals and answer the telephone if we're busy or not here—you'll have to look after the three of them, I'm afraid, and give a hand in the surgery if you have the chance. I'll do the visits and we had better split the night half and half. Which half do you prefer?'

'I don't mind.'

'We'll decide later, shall we?' He smiled suddenly. 'Cressida, did I call you a harridan? I don't know why I said that—I suppose I was tired and worried. I'm sorry. We shall have to work very closely together for the next day or two. Will you mind very much? Working with someone one doesn't like is most unsatisfactory.'

She would have liked to explain to him that she had changed her mind about that; that she liked him after all, indeed, she was begining to wonder why she had disliked him in the first place. True, he vexed her frequently and their relationship was hardly a smooth one and she still wanted to know why he had waited until she had telephoned him before finding out if his partners needed help ... She said sedately: 'I don't mind at all; you're a doctor and I'm a nurse; I don't see that personal feelings enter into it.'

He stared at her rather hard, but she was pouring the coffee and the telephone rang and he went to answer it. 'Old Mijnheer Kulk,' he told her, coming back into the kitchen. 'He's worse and his wife's worried. I'll go now. The number's in the book if you should want me.'

He was businesslike and faintly aloof as he gave her a few directions regarding the patients. Cressida took careful note of them and followed him into the hall, but he went out of the door without saying anything else and the house was suddenly very quiet.

Surprisingly, all three of her patients were sleeping. She tidied the surgery and waiting room with an eye to the morning, laid the table in the kitchen for breakfast and set three trays. It was, surprisingly, not yet midnight and she thought of her bed with longing, wondering how the night could be arranged; if the doctor had to go out on another case, she would have to stay up. She yawned and then became suddenly alert as she heard the car stop before the house. She had been in the sitting-room with the carpet sweeper and a duster; Joukje would have little time for housework if she was to cook the meals, see to the kitchen and do the shopping; besides, having something to do kept her awake. She was on the point of leaving the room when the doctor came in.

'Good lord, haven't you enough to do?' he greeted her. 'Go to bed; I'll keep an eye on things and if there's a call that I think will keep me away for any length of time, I'll call you. You won't need to get up, just stay awake in case the telephone rings. If all's quiet I'll get you up at four o'clock and go to bed myself. Joukje will be here at half past seven, and if she sleeps here it will be of great help.' He yawned hugely and shrugged off his coat. 'Is there any coffee?'

'In the kitchen. I'll get it ...'

'No need. When pushed, I can do quite a lot for myself. Good night, Cressida.'

She went upstairs with mixed feelings, resentful that he was so impatient of her company. True, he had apologised for calling her a harridan, and he had, although she didn't choose to think about it, kissed her—although he had probably been so tired that he didn't know what he was doing—probably he had mistaken her for Mevrouw de Vries. Cressida giggled weakly at that, put her tousled head on the pillow and went fast asleep.

She was awakened at half past three by the doctor; bearing a cup of tea in his hand. 'There's a child in the next village—I shouldn't be long. No need to dress, but do stay awake if you can—you can have another nap when I get back.'

She was still collecting her sleepy thoughts when he went away.

She got up and dressed; whatever he might say, it would be near enough to four o'clock by the time he got back, and time for him to go to bed. She did a quick round of her patients and found Juffrouw Naald awake and worrying about who was to run the house and do the cooking. Cressida had no difficulty in understanding her while she shook up the pillows, took her temperature and gave her a cooling drink and reassured her as best she could in her peculiar Dutch. The news about Joukje seemed to cheer up the housekeeper and when Cressida told her to go to sleep again, she did so almost at once, leaving Cressida free to go downstairs and make a pot of tea against the doctor's return.

He came straight to the kitchen; somehow they had taken it for granted that it should be the focal point of their activities until things got back to normal. 'I told you not to get up?' His voice was impatient and questioning.

'Well, it's almost four o'clock,' she pointed out in a reasonable voice. 'They're all O.K. upstairs; Juffrouw Naald was awake, but she's sleeping now. Is there anything I can do while you're in bed?'

He took the tea she offered him. 'No—you'd better call me if there's anything urgent, though.' He thought for a moment. 'Try and get a couple of hours' sleep after lunch, will you, while I take surgery. If I go to bed now I'll get some sleep before the morning surgery and I may have the chance of a nap during the day.'

She nodded. Neither of them had mentioned the obvious hazard of an emergency call.

They got through the day somehow, and the night

too, and the following day was a pattern of the first. On the third morning Doctor Herrima felt so much better that he had to be restrained from getting up and sitting behind his desk to take his surgery. Juffrouw Naald was better too, only Doctor van Blom was having a fight for it. Cressida, getting up and going to bed when she was told to, no longer cared what time of day it was. She had given up doing anything to her face and although she brushed her hair after a fashion, she tied it back with anything that came handy and let it hang down her back.

The epidemic was on the wane, Doctor van der Teile told her during one of their brief spells of conversation. The hospitals were almost fully staffed again, although there was still no one to spare and no hope of getting help. He spent a good deal of time on the telephone and although she was really too tired to mind, she supposed his calls were to Mevrouw de Vries. Not that she cared, she assured herself in a woolly fashion—it was a pity he wasn't able to go back to wherever he had come from in the first place, for he was poor company. But then so was she; with conversation limited to the state of the patients, the calls to be made and whose turn it was to sleep, it would have been difficult to be anything else. She was a poor substitute indeed for the charming Monique de Vries.

It was that evening, after surgery and the few evening visits that had had to be made, that he told her brusquely that he was going to Groningen. 'Doctor Herrima has a telephone by his bed, he'll deal with anything urgent until I get back. If it's absolutely necessary, you'll have to drive him to the patient—I shall be gone for several hours.'

Cressida stared at him in horror. She had taken a call from Mevrouw de Vries only an hour earlier and fetched him to answer it, and here he was, tearing off to see her, leaving her to hold the fort. And what about Doctor Herrima? He was very much better, but only that morning she had heard Doctor van der Teile tell his partner that the next day was the very earliest that he would allow him to do even an hour's work. 'You can't,' she said loudly, 'you simply can't—can't you make her understand? Doesn't she know ...'

'She?' His voice was icy, but she went on, not really listening. 'Mevrouw de Vries. You forget that I took the call—she's always telephoning you—but must you go? If Doctor Herrima has to go out and gets a chill ... you're being selfish. Besides, you haven't been to bed, you'll go to sleep at the wheel and have an accident and then where shall we be?'

'Far better off without me, I should imagine, judging from your remarks.' His voice was cold and expressionless. 'I'll see you.later.'

She went upstairs to Doctor Herrima and told him firmly that on no account was he to get out of his bed unless she said so, then she went downstairs again to see if there was anything she could do to help Joukje, but everything was under control, and Cressida, feeling strangely restless, wandered round the house, doing quite unnecessary jobs, all the while thinking about Doctor van der Teile. He

85

must be quite hopelessly in love with the glamorous widow—and she *was* glamorous and her clothes had been lovely ... Her head began to ache and she sat down in the great chair in the hall, still thinking about him. He was a selfish man, she had told him so once and she would tell him again. Granted he had worked for three during the last few days, but after the well-organised life he doubtless led, that would do him no harm.

She glanced across at the clock; he had only been gone an hour, but it seemed much longer than that and her headache was getting worse. She had had no fear of getting the 'flu, for she was a healthy girl and sensible; it didn't enter her head now that she might have fallen a victim herself, only as her head got steadily worse and her shivers and aches made themselves felt, she kept her eyes on the clock, wanting Doctor van der Teile to come back, however selfish he was. The clock danced up and down now, but she went on looking at it, as if it were a kind of talisman, determined to keep awake at all costs; there were three people upstairs left in her charge and if Doctor Herrima was called out she had been told to drive him.

'I think I feel very ill,' she said out loud, and took fresh courage as the clock struck the hour; Doctor van der Teile had been gone for almost three hours, he couldn't be much longer now.

CHAPTER FIVE

CRESSIDA wasn't aware that she had closed her eyes, but somehow the clock face had become that of Doctor van der Teile bending over her. He was very close and she noticed in a detached way that his eyes were very blue and bright. She said weakly: 'I'm so sorry, I don't feel very well. I thought I'd wait here for you—you've been gone for such a long time.' She made an enormous effort to be coherent. 'Of course I quite understand why ...'

'Oh, you do, do you? My poor little Cressy.' She had never heard him speak like that before, in such a tender, gentle voice; his arms were gentle too as he picked her up and carried her up to her room.

'Get out of those clothes and into bed, I'll be back in a few minutes.' He sat her on the side of the bed and took off her shoes and untied her hair ribbon before going away. Getting undressed was very tiresome, she discovered, and quite exhausting, but she struggled out of her clothes at last and into a nightdress and crept into bed, shivering and aching and miserable. She hardly noticed when the doctor came back, gave her an injection, took her temperature, felt her pulse and sat her up against her pillows. Joukje came in too with a jug of lemonade and she was made to drink some of it very much against her inclination before she was urged, quite unneccessarily, to go to sleep.

She wakened several times during the night and each time the doctor was there, but towards morning she slipped into a deep slumber and woke from it, hours later, feeling much better. But this time he wasn't there; Monique de Vries was. Cressida, although she still felt awful, was surprised at the surge of ill-feeling she had at the sight of her. 'You shouldn't be here,' she mumbled, ''flu ...'

'I've had it,' the face smiled at her in a most friendly fashion before fading away out of focus. Cressida frowned in her effort to think straight. That was why Doctor van der Teile had rushed off to Groningen and why he had telephoned so often. Just to make sure she asked: 'Do you live in Groningen?'

The pretty face came back and smiled at her. 'Yes, my dear. Do you feel well enough to take your temperature and pulse? Giles told me to ask you to do it if you felt you were able to. I have no idea how to do it—and then you are to have a drink.'

Her temperature was still high, so was her pulse. She watched Monique write them down on a piece of paper, drank the lemonade she was offered and went to sleep again. The doctor's voice roused her. She had no idea how long she had slept and she said hullo without bothering to open her eyes.

'There's a jab coming,' he warned her, and when it was done: 'Headache better? Aches and pains? No pain in your chest?'

She shook her head and opened her eyes reluctantly. 'The others?'

'Doing nicely. Doctor Herrima will be back in a

day or so now, and so will Naaldtje. Doctor van Blom is on the mend too, I'm glad to say.'

'You're tired.' Her head still ached and for the moment she had quite forgotten where she was. 'But you've got Mevrouw de Vries now—I daresay you were very worried about her and you had to come here. No wonder you were so ... you don't even like me ...'

He muttered something in his own language and then said matter-of-factly: 'We none of us could have managed without you, Cressida.'

She pushed the hair away from her face with an impatient hand and looked up at the impassive face above her. 'You called me Cressy.'

His bland expression didn't change. 'Dear me, did I? I shall have to be more careful, shan't I?' A remark which made no sense at all. 'Go to sleep now, there's a good girl, you're going to feel a lot better when you wake up.'

And she did. Her head was clear and she hardly ached at all. It was bliss to feel normal again—well, nearly normal. She stretched luxuriously, turned over and went to sleep again.

When she woke it was to waning daylight with a brisk wind howling round the square and she lay for a moment, astonished to think that she had slept for so long; she was still a little hazy, but she must have been lying there for almost forty-eight hours. And now she felt clear-headed again and very hungry. She got out of bed, disregarding the jelly-like feeling in her legs, put on her dressing gown and slippers and went out of her room, intent on finding food. The house was quiet although she could hear voices somewhere, and from the top of the staircase she could see that the big clock in the hall showed the hour of half past three. Holding to the banisters because her legs weren't quite her own yet, she had to pass the sitting-room door to do this and as it was half open she peered in.

Doctor van der Teile was there, standing by the window, and Monique de Vries was with him. Neither of them saw her, which was a good thing, because Monique had her head on his shoulder and his arm was round her. Cressida backed away; one didn't encroach on such scenes, it was like reading someone else's letters. She went slowly back to her room again, quite forgetful of her hunger, and the tears streamed down her face although she had no idea why she was crying. She got back into bed and mopped her face and tried to go to sleep again, quite unsuccessfully, and presently they both came in quietly, and although she had her eyes shut it was no use, for he said at once: 'You're not asleep—and you've been crying. Why?'

She said the first thing which came into her head, 'I'm hungry,' and wondered uneasily if he would notice that her dressing gown, which had been hanging behind the door, was now thrown down anyhow on a chair. Apparently he hadn't, for he smiled a little as he took her pulse and asked his companion to see that Joukje got a tray ready. 'Something light —soup, thin bread and butter—there are some grapes too—oh, and a pot of tea.'

Monique went away and he sat down beside the

bed. 'Now tell me why you've been crying,' he invited her gently.

'I don't know,' and she didn't. 'I just felt miserable, but I really don't know why.'

He went to stand by the window, his hands in his pockets, jingling his loose change. He wasn't looking at her, but at the grey day outside. 'You must stay in bed for another two days,' he told her. 'You are making a good recovery, but you were tired out and we'll not take any chances.'

'I feel perfectly able to get up.'

'Yes? I see that you have already done so. Very foolish of you, Cressida.'

So he had noticed. She asked quickly: 'How are the doctors and Juffrouw Naald?'

'Naaldtje is better, she threw it off very well, Doctor Herrima is just about ready to get into harness again, but Doctor van Blom will have to take things easy for another few days—his chest hasn't quite cleared.'

'Will you stay here until he is better?'

'No, I can't do that. As soon as Doctor Herrima is able to carry on I must return.'

Cressida sat up a little higher in bed. 'Is—is Mevrouw de Vries staying here?'

'Yes, but I shall take her back with me when I go.'

He turned round and came back to stand by the bed. He looked very tired and she wondered how much sleep he had been getting; it wouldn't be enough. 'You must be longing to get back,' she said flatly.

He smiled down at her. 'Yes, I am most anxious to return.'

'All your private patients,' she muttered peevishly.

He appeared not to notice her peevishness, for he agreed placidly, 'As you say, all my private patients.' He looked over his shoulder as the door was opened and Mevrouw de Vries came in with a tray. 'And here is your tray—I'll look in later.' With a careless nod he had gone.

Cressida recovered quickly; she was a strong girl, not given to illness, and by the end of the next two days she was sitting out of bed, and when no one was about, pottering downstairs to visit Juffrouw Naald in her kitchen, for although that lady was by no means quite well again, nothing would prevent her from overseeing Joukje's efforts. And Doctor Herrima had taken his afternoon surgery that afternoon and had signified his intention of resuming his work in the morning. His partner was convalescing but improving so rapidly now that things would be back to normal in a few days. Their senior partner, Doctor van Blom had told her, would be able to return to his own home on the following day. 'We shall miss him,' he declared. 'What a task he took upon himself, and at the expense of his own patients too, not to mention his own peace of mind.'

Cressida had wondered what his peace of mind could have to do with it, but she didn't like to ask, and the doctor went on: 'We shall miss Monique too —hard work is hardly her *forte*, so it is all the more appreciated. And you, my dear Cressida, we shall never be able to thank you enough,' he beamed at her. 'I do not know what we should have done without you. However, now you will be able to return to your typewriter.'

She was sitting with Doctor van Blom the following afternoon, reading over some of his manuscript to refresh his memory about several alterations, when Doctor van der Teile came in. He was dressed for the road, and Cressida, who hadn't seen him all day, presumed that he was back from the afternoon round. She was quite right, he was; he was also on the point of departure.

He talked with his partner for a few minutes, uttered a few commonplace remarks to her, wished her goodbye with casual politeness, and went. She hadn't said a word and her goodbye, muttered in surprise, was lost to him, for he was already half way down the stairs by the time she had her mouth open to speak.

'Go and wave from the window,' suggested her patient. 'Monique came to see me while you were in the study; she had been looking for you so that she might say goodbye. She left a number of kind messages for you and hopes to meet you again soon.'

'I bet she does,' thought Cressida vulgarly, and went obediently to look out into the square below. Mevrouw de Vries was already in the Bentley and she looked up and waved and blew a kiss when she saw Cressida and then spoke to someone standing, presumably, in the doorway. Doctor van der Teile came into view seconds later and looked up too. But he neither waved nor smiled and he certainly didn't blow a kiss, only stared up at her, looking vaguely irritable as though he hadn't wanted to do it.

Cressida stared back at him; he was going away and she didn't want him to; she wanted him to stay for ever; better still, she would have liked to turn the elegant Monique out of the Bentley and take her place. It was, she told herself gloomily, the silliest time in which to discover that she loved him.

She turned away from the window abruptly, unable to watch him get into his car and drive away. And it's not just away from here, she thought sadly, it's away from me, even if I see him again—and he had said goodbye as though he was pleased to say it.

'Giles has gone?' asked Doctor van Blom from his chair.

'Yes, he's gone.' Her voice, regrettably, shook just a little.

Another few days and they were back—almost—in their usual way of life once more. True, Joukje still did the lion's share of the work while Juffrouw Naald confined her activities to cooking and the supervision of the house cleaning, made easier by Joukje's younger sister, Trusje, who came in to help each day. And Doctor Herrima took his surgery and did the visits with Cressida driving him, and after a few days, Doctor van Blom got into his clothes and insisted on doing at least one surgery a day.

In between these activities, Cressida started her typing once more, working until quite late at night and taking the manuscript to bed with her and working on that too, until she couldn't keep her eyes open any longer. It stopped her from thinking, something which she wished to avoid for the next week or so. 'Out of sight, out of mind,' she consoled herself, knowing that there wasn't a word of truth in it. But she did try very hard, taking herself for a long walk each day, sandwiched in between the surgery and the rounds; it was astonishing what a great deal of ground one could cover in an hour, and if one walked fast enough one had little time to think ... all the same, she wakened each morning to her unhappy thoughts and went down to the study with such a pale face that Doctor van Blom wondered aloud if he was asking too much of her. 'This wretched 'flu,' he exclaimed, 'you haven't recovered from it, Cressida, and I'm working you too hard—I'm working myself too hard too; it will do me good to have a day free from the book, and you must have a day to yourself.'

It was the last thing she wanted, for what would she do? Go to Groningen, she suspected, and walk the streets, hoping that she would come face to face with Giles van der Teile. She refused politely and applied herself even more zealously to her typing, pointing out that they had lost precious time and she would need every minute she could spare in order to have the book ready by the date the publishers had set.

It was the following afternoon that Doctor van der Teile came. Doctor Herrima had finished surgery and refused her offer to drive him on his rounds, now considerably lighter. Doctor van Blom was happily engaged on the final polishing of the

95

last chapter and she was back at her typewriter. But she had barely started when the front door was opened and shut with something of a thud, and Doctor van der Teile came into the room, bringing with him the cold air from outside and a feeling of strong purpose.

Cressida hadn't expected to see him, but she had been thinking of him constantly, so that she went quite pale and then flushed a little, making her lovely face even lovelier. He gave her a casual 'Hullo,' and an equally casual glance before addressing himself to his colleagues in his own language, and she bent over her typewriter again and missed his intent gaze upon her even though he was engaged in conversation with Doctor van Blom.

He stared at her in the manner of a man who couldn't see enough of her and spoke abruptly in English. 'Doctor van Blom thinks that you should have a break from work. You have been doing too much and you're barely out of bed.'

These words caused her to stop in the middle of a sentence and look at him. 'Me? Working too hard? I'm not!'

'Probably you're unaware of it,' he said smoothly. 'Why not come back with me to Groningen and have dinner there?' He smiled suddenly. 'There is someone who would like to meet you.'

'Meet me?' asked Cressida. She felt that her conversation hardly sparkled, but she couldn't help that; she was still wondering why on earth he should bother himself to ask her out—and who would want to meet her?

'A splendid idea.' Doctor van Blom for once spoke firmly. 'There is no typing for you to do until I have re-read this chapter. Run along now, Cressida, and put on your coat and go with Giles.'

He gave her a fatherly nod, his cheerful face full of benevolence, pleased to be the instrument, in part, of an evening out for her, so that to disappoint him would have been out of the question—or so she told herself as she did her hair and her face, and then, warmly wrapped against the cold dusk, went downstairs to join Doctor van der Teile.

They occupied the journey to Groningen with polite conversation, casual on the doctor's part, and rather stiff on her own; she was so afraid that he would discover how she felt about him that she leaned over backwards to appear cool and casual and utterly impervious to his charm, but all she succeeded in doing was to utter a series of commonplace remarks hardly remarkable for their interest. But her companion, beyond a faint twitch of the lip, seemed unaware of this, blandly matching her efforts with even more commonplace replies, so that by the time they reached the city she was quite illogically put out with him. He could at least talk about something interesting. She asked a thought snappishly: 'Where are we going?'

For answer he swung the car between open iron gates and drew up before what was obviously a hospital entrance. 'In here,' he told her briefly, and before she could question him further, he had guided her inside, into a lift and out of it again, down a long quiet corridor lined with doors, and finally, through the last door at its end.

The room was small but pleasant, with pretty curtains, a comfortable chair and a polished wood floor, and there were flowers everywhere; they formed a frame for the occupant of the bed, a middle-aged lady with handsome features and a commanding appearance despite the fact that she had been, and still was, Cressida could see, quite ill. She was carefully made up and her hair was done in what Cressida called to herself a continental knot. She wore a high-necked long-sleeved nightdress of some fine silk in a pretty shade of blue, exquisitely embroidered and trimmed with lace—the blue matched her eyes exactly, eyes as astonishingly blue as her son's.

'Dear Giles,' she greeted him, 'how nice to see you—and you have brought Miss Bingley to visit me.' She offered a cheek for his kiss and held out a beautifully manicured hand to Cressida, who shook it gently with a polite murmur.

'Of course Giles would not have told you that he was bringing you to see me,' went on his mother in effortless English. 'His mind is almost wholly occupied with other people's chests, you know, and he has no time for the niceties—only I very much wanted to meet you, my dear—you see I heard all about the magnificent way in which you coped with this wretched 'flu. Giles thought of a dozen reasons why you wouldn't want to come, but I think that you would not mind satisfying the whim of an old lady?'

This description of herself made Cressida smile; anyone less elderly, even when recovering from whatever it was that had laid her low, would be hard to find; she fancied that the lady lying in bed would probably ignore illness and even when she had succumbed to it, had made up her mind to get better, whatever anyone else thought.

'I don't mind in the least,' she told her. 'In fact, it's very nice to meet someone who speaks English —the doctors do, of course, but not Juffrouw Naald —oh, and of course Doctor van der Teile ...'

The blue eyes twinkled. 'I expect you both had far too much to do to have the time to get to know each other,' suggested Mevrouw van der Teile. 'Giles, go and look at some X-rays or something while I talk to Cressida—I may call you that?' She smiled at her son. 'Come back in half an hour—no, don't frown, I know I'm not allowed to have visitors for more than fifteen minutes.'

'Knowing you, Mama,' he observed smilingly, 'I imagine you entertain whoever you wish for as long as you wish.' He walked to the door. 'Fifteen minutes, then.' He gave Cressida a cool nod and went out, shutting the door gently behind him.

'The dear boy,' remarked his mother fondly, and glanced at Cressida. 'Always so busy, you know. His practice—a very large one—and the hospital here and beds at Leeuwarden too, and then his partnership with Doctor Herrima and Doctor van Blom —not a real partnership, but during the Occupation they tried to help his father and when Giles heard of it he swore that he would help them in his turn.

99

He is what you call a sleeping partner.' She paused. 'And now of course his clinic is running successfully ...' She paused again, invitingly, and Cressida asked, inevitably. 'What clinic?'

'Oh, hasn't he told you about it?' Mevrouw van der Teile gave her an innocent look. 'Perhaps I should not do so, but you are a nurse, are you not, and I am sure that you would be interested to hear about it. He started it four years ago, for he felt that the chest cases which he saw in hospital needed more specialised care when they returned home; despite health visitors and reminders from the hospital, so many of them didn't bother to return for check-ups, which meant that their stay in hospital was so often useless, often they didn't bother to see their own doctor either. But strangely, the clinic is a great success, possibly because it is in a part of the city where living conditions are not ideal even though modern flats are being built—it is, as it were, just round the corner, if you see what I mean. A man with bronchitis or asthma might not bother himself to come across the city to visit the hospital, but he would slip round to the clinic one evening —and now the local doctors with patients unwilling to go to hospital for an examination have taken to sending them in for Giles to see. He does it in his spare time, of course ...' She paused to get her breath and Cressida said gently: 'Should you be talking so much, Mevrouw?'

'No, my dear, but I wanted you to know. I'm surprised that Giles hasn't said anything to you about it—but then, very few people know about it, he prefers it that way.'

'Well, he doesn't know me very well,' said Cressida. 'There's no reason why he should tell me anything about himself.'

'I don't suppose he told you that I became tiresomely ill on the very day you telephoned him for help?'

'Oh, dear,' said Cressida, and remembered all the awful things she had said to him about being a well-heeled consultant and not pulling his weight. 'No, he didn't—I had no idea ... that's why he went to Groningen when he should have gone to bed. He didn't say a word ...' She coloured faintly. 'Well, as a matter of fact, he did say that he had to keep a date with a lady ...'

His mother laughed. 'I despair of him,' she declared, not sounding in the least despairing. 'And now tell me, do you like working for Doctor van Blom?'

'Very much. It's a change from nursing and he is very kind, so is Doctor Herrima—and Doctor van der Teile,' Cressida added hastily, and caught his parent's eye. 'I—that is, we ...' She stopped and tried again. 'He doesn't like me, I think, although he's always very ... very ...'

Mevrouw van der Teile was examining the pink nails of one hand and interrupted her without looking up. 'And you, my dear—you dislike him?'

'No.' Cressida struggled to think of something suitable to say and could think of nothing, so she filled the silence with: 'I don't suppose I shall be here much longer, the book is going very well and it's almost finished ...' She paused and let out a small thankful sigh as the door opened and Giles came in and his mother said at once: 'We have had a most delightful talk—I have been telling Cressida about your clinic and I daresay you will be very annoyed at that, but I quite thought that you would have told her already. Are you very vexed?'

Cressida took a quick peep; he wasn't vexed, he was in a cold rage about it. 'Not in the least,' he assured his mother with untruthful, icy politeness, 'although I cannot conceive of what interest it may be to Cressida.'

His mother ignored this. 'Well, why don't you take her to see it?'

He frowned. 'Perhaps—at some future date.'

'This evening, Giles—why not?' Her eyes held his own frosty ones. 'So nice to share your interests with someone who understands them,' she remarked in dulcet tones.

Cressida, watching him, gave way to a desire to stoke his rage a little. How tiresome he was, and how she loved him. 'I'll not tell anyone,' she assured him in kindly tones, and was rewarded by a glacial look and: 'I shall be delighted to take you —we can perhaps arrange a date later on.'

After she was back in England. 'Why not this evening, Giles?' His mother's voice, still dulcet, was persistent too. Only good manners, Cressida decided, prevented him from grinding his splendid teeth.

'Oh, yes, please,' she chimed in, and added a

sweet smile, flicking her long lashes down on to her cheeks and then opening her eyes wide at him. She was pleased to see that he showed unwilling interest even though he was still in a rage.

The polite chill of his voice froze her bones. 'Very well, but I doubt if you will find it interesting. Shall we have dinner first?' His tone implied that dining with her would be a duty.

'If you like.' If he wasn't going to ask her nicely then she wasn't going to answer nicely either. She went on: 'I'm sure I shall find this clinic very interesting, although you don't seem to think so. I'm very surprised, I thought you were just a consultant.'

He was arrogant now as well as angry, looking down his nose at her. Cressida wondered why she was being so beastly when what she really wanted to do was throw her arms round his neck and tell him he was everything she had ever hoped for in a man. His mother broke the small silence. 'Run along, then, my dears,' she commanded, and offered her cheek for her son's kiss and then took Cressida's hand, smiling at her. She was weary now, but she was a woman who had no intention of giving way to anything as unimportant as weariness. 'We shall see each other again.'

The doctor opened the door with exaggerated politeness and with a final nod to his mother followed Cressida into the corridor. They didn't speak in the corridor or in the lift. It wasn't until they were sitting side by side in the Bentley that he remarked bitingly, 'You are a scheming minx, Cressida, and clever with it. I don't know how you managed to worm so much out of my mother, but you succeeded very well. It was—unworthy of you.'

He started the car and drove to the hospital gates where he was forced to pull up until he could slide into the traffic of the main road. It gave Cressida the chance to get her door open; she had one leg out before he leaned across, swept her back in with one arm, fastened her safety belt and closed the door.

'Of all the rude, self-opinionated, unpleasant men ...! I will not have dinner with you!'

'No? Perhaps that wouldn't be such a bad idea in the circumstances. We will go straight to the clinic.'

'I do not want ...' she began, and was interrupted by his smooth: 'You're going, whether you want to or not,' and when she stole a glance at his profile she was surprised to see that he looked amused.

He swung the car into the traffic and was fully occupied in driving it through a chain of side streets which seemed to go on for ever, until he finally stopped in a narrow, shabby square. Without a word he opened her door, ushered her out of the car and across the pavement, through a door and into a long whitewashed passage from which led a great many doors. Cressida could hear voices from behind them and one was opened and a man in a white coat came out, walking towards them. When he caught sight of them he hurried to meet them and spoke to the doctor with some surprise. After a few moments' talk, Doctor van der Teile said briefly: 'This is Jan Vinke—he works here.'

He waited while she shook hands and then

marched her on. 'What does he do?' she asked him, refusing to be crushed by his manner.

'He is one of the nurses.'

'How many work here?'

'Four.'

'Is it a large clinic?'

'You shall see for yourself.' He opened a door and urged her in so smartly that she paused to eye him severely. 'You're in a very nasty temper,' she told him, 'and I refuse to be bullied around after the quite beastly things you said to me just now. In any case, your high-handed ways cut no ice with me.' She turned her back on him then, because when one loved someone it was really very difficult to be angry with them for more than a few minutes at a time.

He took no notice of her at all; the door shut behind them and she found herself in a large room crowded with people sitting on benches. She was led between them, the doctor nodding here and there as they went until they reached a door at the further end which he opened. There was another man here, sitting behind a desk, writing furiously, but he jumped up as they went in and broke into speech.

He looked rather nice, youngish and thickset and very fair. He seemed pleased to see the doctor, although a little in awe of him. Cressida, watching them talk, saw the icy blandness go from his face and sighed to see it reappear as he introduced his colleague.

'Cressida, this is Doctor Felix de Boer.'

The younger man shook hands with every appearance of friendliness and said in excellent English: 'I am enchanted; we do not often have visits from young ladies of such beauty. You are interested in the clinic?'

'Yes, I am, but I know almost nothing about it.'

'I cannot suppose that it can interest you in the least,' interrupted Doctor van der Teile, faintly bored.

'Oh, come now, Doctor,' said the other man, 'you're saying that because you dislike people knowing of your work here. Miss Bingley, I could tell you ...'

'Oh, do,' urged Cressida, and smiled sweetly at Giles' handsome face and got no response at all. She didn't give up easily, but addressed him directly: 'How many patients do you have, and do you work here every evening?'

He spoke repressively. 'We have about ninety patients each week and we open three evenings in the week. None of us works full time. And now that you have had your wish and have seen all that you came to see, I think we might go.'

'You're very impatient,' she smiled again at him and he looked annoyed. 'I haven't seen anything at all, really. Do you share the work?' she asked Doctor de Boer.

'There is another doctor—we each do an evening, but there are often extra clinics.'

She turned to Doctor van der Teile again. 'It must give you a very long working day,' she said, and he nodded curtly without speaking. It was like getting blood from a stone, and suddenly she felt beaten. She said on a sigh: 'I'm wasting your time —your whole evening, in fact. I'm sorry.' She held out a hand to Doctor de Boer. 'I mustn't keep you from your patients. I have enjoyed meeting you. Thank you.'

She went through the door, not looking to see if Giles was behind her. He was. He opened the car door for her without speaking and she asked in a sober little voice: 'Will you please take me home?' and choked back sudden anger at his bland: 'With pleasure, Cressida.'

He had nothing more to say until he drew up before his partners' house and, rather to her surprise, went inside with her. In the hall he remarked pleasantly, 'I hope you don't mind going to bed supperless, Cressida.'

It was more than enough. 'I'm famished!' she told him in a shrill voice which threatened to become a wail. 'And I think you're quite— quite ...'

'Beastly?'

She flew upstairs and banged her door behind her, then tore off her clothes and had a bath, crying all the time. Then she brushed her hair, secured her dressing gown firmly round her person and went stealthily out of her room again, into the silent house and down the stairs. Everyone would be sleeping—they still kept early hours after the last exhausting fortnight. She padded to the kitchen, poured herself a mug of milk, cut herself a massive slice of bread, buttered it, laid cheese thickly upon it, and bore her supper back to her room. She paused at the foot of the stairs to take a bite, for her hunger had got the better of her. She was savouring it blissfully when a faint sound made her look round. Doctor van der Teile was standing across the hall, watching her. Before she could speak, he had reached her and taken the milk and bread from her, setting them carefully on the stairs. 'I cannot think of anything to say,' he muttered. 'This will have to do instead.'

She felt his arms around her as he bent to kiss her, then picked up her supper and put it back into her hands. Cressida could think of nothing to say, for she could hardly tell him that his kiss had been quite out of the ordinary and that she had enjoyed it very much, and to wish him a prosaic good night didn't seem to fit the occasion. She went back upstairs without looking at him, shut the door, softly this time, and got into bed to enjoy the remains of her supper and ponder the doctor's behaviour. She had, until now, almost given up hope of his liking her, but now she wasn't sure and hope surged higher within her with every minute, only to be quenched by the thought that he couldn't really like her; hadn't he refused to give her the dinner he had invited her to share with him—not invited, either—insisted, now she came to think of it.

She put down her mug, disposed of the last morsel of bread and lay down. She was still worrying away at the puzzle like a dog with a bone, when she heard the Bentley slide past under her window and gather speed as it tore into the night.

CHAPTER SIX

CRESSIDA spent most of the next day wondering how she should behave towards Giles van der Teile when she saw him next, but she need not have worried; there was no sign of him, nor on the following day either. He was due to see some patients on the day after that; Doctor Herrima had mentioned it at breakfast, a statement which had caused her to make a great many mistakes in her typing that morning, and sent her upstairs before lunch to re-do her face and pile her shining hair even more neatly than it was already, and this was a waste too, for at lunch she was told—by Doctor van Blom this time—that their partner had been called away to Utrecht and wouldn't be back in time to see any of his patients that afternoon.

Cressida swallowed disappointment with her soup and spent the whole afternoon working with a ferocity which was quite remarkable. At this rate, Doctor van Blom told her happily, the book would be ready in plenty of time to meet the publisher's date, and he added: 'But I shall be sorry too, my dear, for we have enjoyed having you here with us, and you have been invaluable, for you are such a sensible young woman and seem able to turn your hand to anything.'

She thanked him for the compliment and wished

for the hundredth time that her command of the Dutch language was sufficient for her to suggest that she might remain with them as a surgery nurse and secretary, for they certainly needed someone ... she had done her best to pick up a few basic sentences, and with Juffrouw Naald's help and the aid of a dictionary, she hadn't done so badly, but she doubted if she knew enough to cope with the daily demands of a busy surgery.

She had managed well enough during the brief period when they had all had 'flu, but that had been rather a different matter. It just wouldn't work, she admitted regretfully, and turned back resolutely to her desk, where she stayed, pausing only for a cup of tea. By dinner time she was quite worn out, which was a good thing, for she slept the moment her head touched the pillow. But her waking thought was of Giles; it was stupid, she told herself crossly, that she was unable to clear her head of the man; it was a complete waste of time thinking about him. He was rude and arrogant and she suspected that she amused him, although she wasn't sure why—and yet he was the only man in her life and she knew that there would never be another. He could be as cross as two sticks and look down his nose at her and not care if she went supperless to bed; it made no difference.

She dressed and went down to the study, where she attacked the last chapter with Doctor van Blom, and became so immersed in it that they were late for breakfast, and because there were a great many patients in the surgery that morning, she helped there before going back to the study.

They were all a little tired by lunchtime, but there was no surgery that afternoon, so that the two doctors could have an hour or two's leisure. Cressida covered her typewriter and decided reluctantly that she would go for a walk. It was a cheerless sort of day, but the fresh air would do her good. She put the study to rights, then went without haste into the hall and came face to face with Doctor van der Teile.

He had just arrived, for he was still wearing his car coat and was in the act of stripping off his gloves. He said pleasantly, 'Hullo—I thought we might go out for lunch.'

She wished with all her heart that she had on something more glamorous than the thick brown tweed skirt and its toning jumper. She hadn't done her face for ages, either. 'Why?' she asked.

He laughed. 'Let us say an impulse, Cressida, even a wish to make amends for your lack of supper the other evening.'

'How kind,' her voice was a little too loud, 'but I don't think I can manage it.'

He raised his brows. 'And what exactly does that mean?'

She stood in front of him, stubbornly refusing to give in to a weak desire to say yes. 'It's a polite way of saying I don't want to have lunch with you.'

This time his laugh was a great bellow. 'Don't be mulish, Cressida—and you're not usually so polite ...'

'I should have to change.'

His surprise was genuine. 'Why? You look quite all right to me. You'll need a coat, though.'

Men! thought Cressida peevishly, and wondered if he was as uncritical of Monique de Vries, and doubted it. She was on the point of saying firmly that she wouldn't go when she caught his eye.

'Run along, there's a dear girl. I'll give you five minutes—ten if you insist on changing everything.' He grinned suddenly. 'And don't tell me that that won't be long enough; looks like yours don't need fussing over.'

Her instant pleasure at this remark was cut to the ground by his: 'Monique considers you to be one of the prettiest girls she has ever seen.'

So it hadn't been his own opinion, but something Monique had said. Cressida looked away so that he shouldn't see her face. 'I'll be less than five minutes,' she told him quietly, and sped up to her room. There was no point in spending more time than that on her person; he wasn't going to look at her, not really look—she didn't think that he ever had, or he might have thought up a compliment for himself instead of relying on his Monique ... She tugged on her coat, rammed the fur cap on to her head and snatched up her handbag and gloves, all the while fighting a strong impulse to wear her elderly mac and a headscarf—she didn't even bother to powder her nose.

On her way downstairs she wondered what was his real reason for inviting her out to lunch, and she was to discover that soon enough. They were in the car, speeding towards Groningen, when Doctor van der Teile remarked casually, 'My mother would like you to visit her again—I thought perhaps after lunch? I have a couple of patients to see in the hospital; I could leave you with her and pick you up afterwards—you're not committed to anything this afternoon?'

'Only my typing,' she told him dryly.

'Ah—yes, I hadn't forgotten, but Doctor van Blom tells me that you haven't been taking nearly enough time off for the last few days and that you're well ahead with the book.'

He was cutting the ground from beneath her feet, inch by inch. 'I shall be delighted to visit your mother, Doctor van der Teile.'

'Giles.'

'Giles, then.'

They were in the city by now and he drew up presently in an old narrow street leading off one of the main squares, in front of a gabled house so discreetly converted into a restaurant that it was difficult to see, at first glance, that it was just that.

Inside it was warm and gently lighted against the winter's day outside, and they were shown at once to a snugly placed table by one of the windows in the oak-panelled room. Cressida, as she sat down, noted with some chagrin that the women at the tables around them were smartly dressed, most of them with fur coats thrown back over their chairs. She allowed the waiter to take the tweed and threw a reproachful look at her companion, who said at once: 'You don't have to look like that.'

'Like what?'

'As though you are wearing all the wrong clothes. Believe me, when a girl is as pretty as you are, you could get away with wearing the tablecloth.'

She wondered if Monique de Vries had said that too. 'Two compliments within the hour,' she observed. 'Thank you.'

He only smiled a little. 'What would you like to drink?' he asked. 'There's a rather nice dry sherry ...'

She agreed to that, not knowing much about drinks, and fell to studying the menu card. It was written in French, which was a good thing, because if it had been in Dutch he would have had to translate it to her. She was searching for something not too wildly expensive when the matter was taken out of her hands, her companion suggesting that she might like the *Truite Saumonée au Champagne*, with the *Pâté Maison* to precede it. 'Unless you care to join me in an underdone steak?' he added, and when she wrinkled her nose: 'I thought not, but I can recommend the trout.'

Cressida thought privately that at that price anyone would be safe to recommend it, and when the pâté came, polished it off delicately with a splendid appetite before tackling the trout. Giles had done right to order it for her, for it was delicious; she ate every morsel and enjoyed it while they talked of nothing in particular. Her companion appeared to be on his best behaviour, too, for he said nothing to annoy her to which she could take exception. Indeed, he put himself out to entertain her and it was impossible to discover if he was enjoying her company or not. Certainly if he disliked her, he was concealing it very well; on the other hand he showed no partiality for her either.

She accepted his suggestion to try the chocolate soufflé, and allowed her glass to be refilled with the Sauterne he had chosen, for after all, she would probably not eat another meal like the present one for some time—perhaps never.

The early afternoon was already darkening as they left the restaurant, but she hardly noticed; she was enjoying herself—she wouldn't see very much more of Giles after this outing together; she was going to extract every scrap of pleasure she could from it. Never mind what he thought of her, just being with him was a happiness she had never expected or imagined. Probably because of the Sauterne, her face was a little flushed and her eyes sparkled, so that when they entered his mother's room that lady greeted them with: 'I can see that you have been enjoying yourselves, my dear. Cressida, come and sit down and talk to me while Giles sees those patients of his.'

So Cressida sat, answering the questions put to her by the formidable lady in the bed; for she was formidable and accustomed to getting her own way without doubt, taking it for granted that when she wanted something done, it would be attended to immediately and without question, and yet she was charming too and, Cressida suspected, very lovable. She wondered how mother and son got on, for they both had strong personalities, and as though the invalid had been reading her thoughts, she remarked in her commanding voice: 'Giles and I are devoted to one another, you know. His father died some years ago—he was in a concentration camp during World War Two, and although he survived it, it killed him eventually. He was a doctor too, and a brilliant one; he was also a man of iron will with a fierce temper.' Her face softened. 'We were ideally happy, which is strange, because I am strong-willed too. Giles is mostly his father, I think,' she smiled, 'especially the fierce temper, although he seldom allows it to show, but he can be—difficult at times.' She added innocently: 'I expect he has annoyed you?'

'Yes,' said Cressida.

Her companion nodded. 'I know—he can be so vexing that one could shake him. Monique has said it of him many times.'

'They're old friends?' It hurt to keep her voice casual, but she managed it.

'Oh, very old. She is in Paris for a week or two buying clothes. She is the kind of woman who has to go to Paris for them.' There was a slight edge to Mevrouw van der Teile's voice.

So that was why he had asked her out to lunch, thought Cressida painfully; he had been at a loose end. She wondered when he was going to marry Monique and longed to ask, but pride tied her tongue. She observed brightly: 'It must be fun to buy things in Paris, but I've seen some lovely clothes here—in Amsterdam and Groningen.'

'Den Haag,' stated the older lady categorically, 'that is the place to go for clothes. If ever you should wish to shop there, let me know, Cressida, and I will tell you the names of the best places.'

'Thank you, Mevrouw,' said Cressida composedly, 'but I don't expect to buy clothes of that kind.'

'One never knows,' stated Mevrouw van der Teile, and she uttered the trite phrase with pleased emphasis, just as though she had invented it for herself. 'You dress well, child.'

'Thank you, Mevrouw.' The conversation, Cressida discovered uneasily, was centred upon herself. In a moment her companion would be starting on her round of questions again. She said hastily: 'I expect you are looking forward to leaving here—have you any idea when you are to go home?'

'I spoke to the doctors this morning,' observed Mevrouw van der Teile, and Cressida was quite sure that was exactly what she had done, flattening out the poor men before they could get behind their professional faces. 'I wished to know exactly what they thought, and provided they have told me the truth, I expect to leave here within the week. One must naturally allow for unexpected events.'

Like collapsed lungs, heart failure, pneumonia again, bronchitis ... all nasty complications which could follow a severe chest infection and all presumably lumped together in the lady's mind as events. Cressida had a sudden ridiculous urge to take the formidable lady in her arms and give her a hug. 'I'm sure that D ... Giles will see that you get home just as soon as possible,' she said soothingly. 'I know you aren't his patient, but he has probably been consulted about you.'

His mother nodded regally. 'Indeed, yes. Any other man than Giles would have had a swelled head and an exaggerated opinion of himself by now—he has many faults, but thank heaven conceit is not one of them.' She coughed. 'Do you like my son, Cressida?'

Cressida choked, went pink and opened and closed her mouth like a beautiful fish suddenly finding itself without water. 'I ... I ...' she began, knowing that she would have to say something under those compelling eyes, and then let out a long soundless sigh as the door opened and the object of their conversation walked in.

He sat down at once and engaged them in a conversation which allowed of no personalities at all, and presently, when Cressida suggested that she should perhaps be going, he acquiesced with a readiness which quite shook her. But he was still the pleasant, perfectly mannered host, waiting while she bade his mother goodbye and then ushering her out to the car without hurrying her. It seemed to take no time at all to reach the village, but as he had the habit of driving fast, she could hardly attribute his speed to a wish to be rid of her company as soon as possible. Besides, he maintained a steady flow of small talk all the way, which gave her no clue as to his real feelings. He went into the house with her, cut short the polite speech of thanks she was on the point of making, and swept her rather impatiently into Doctor van Blom's empty study.

'What have I done?' he wanted to know, and when she didn't answer from sheer surprise: 'Or what haven't I done? Or what have I said—or perhaps my mama has said?'

'Nothing.'

He addressed the room at large. 'Why does a woman always say "nothing" to a man while all the time she is only waiting for the right moment to pour the vials of her rage upon his unfortunate head?'

'You seem to know a lot about it.' Cressida had taken off her cap and was standing half turned away from him.

'Of course I do. I have a mother, have I not? and over the years I have had a number of girl-friends, you know.'

'And one in particular,' snapped Cressida, quite unable to hold her tongue.

He gave her a long, thoughtful look. 'As you say, one girl in particular.'

She went to her desk and uncovered her typewriter; it gave her something to do. 'Thank you for my delightful lunch, and I enjoyed meeting your mother again.'

It was disobliging of him not to answer her. In the silence which followed she sought desperately for a graceful phrase with which to fill it. Her head filled immediately with snatches of song, the first lines of a dozen hymns, even a half forgotten recipe for bread, but not a single graceful phrase. She gave him a look of deep exasperation and he said, half smiling, 'You're not going to tell me, are you, Cressida? Not now, at any rate.'

'Not ever,' she assured him.

'That sounds like a very long time. No matter. I am, when it suits me, a very patient man.'

He wasn't smiling any more, he looked to be on the point of saying something else, but the door opened at that moment and Doctor van Blom came in. Cressida slipped away to her room and stayed there prudently until, peeping from her window, she saw the Bentley slide away from the front door.

For the rest of the day she worked for two; if she kept on at the rate she was going, the book would be finished well in advance of the publisher's date, and that might be a good thing, for then she could go back to England and forget all about Giles; it didn't seem likely that she would, but she would have to try, and pride might help her. Her heart told her that she had no pride where Giles was concerned, but common sense got the better of her feelings; she would finish the book as quickly as she could and leave. She spent the next two days typing assiduously, but on the third morning Doctor van Blom, supported by his partner, decreed that she was to have a day off; to sit at a desk all day was not good for her, they pronounced. The book was almost done now, there was no longer any need for her to work so hard—besides, the weather had turned cold and frosty, ideal for a day out. Doctor Herrima mentioned that he was going to Leeuwarden and wouldn't it be a good idea if she were to telephone Harriet and invite herself to lunch?

Cressida hesitated, and Doctor van Blom said slyly: 'As a matter of fact, Giles was there yesterday and she asked particularly after you and asked if you couldn't spend a day there, and he suggested that you might like to lunch with them today—Doctor Herrima will drop you off ...'

'Well,' said Cressida on an indignant breath, 'of all the ...!' She didn't finish the sentence, because her two kindly companions were looking at her expectantly, delighted with their little plot, waiting to be praised and thanked.

She did both, generously, and watched their smiles. They really were two of the nicest, kindest men she had ever met. She left them to fetch her outdoor things; Doctor van Blom reaching for the telephone to tell Harriet that she was on her way, and Doctor Herrima making for his car.

'You're sure you can manage?' she asked Doctor van Blom anxiously as she arrived in the hall again, dressed for outdoors.

'Of course, my dear—there is only the morning surgery today, as you know, and Doctor Herrima will be back here for lunch. Have a good time—Friso will drive you back this evening.'

He went with her to the door, settled her into the car beside his partner and stood waving goodbye until they were out of sight.

She sat quietly beside Doctor Herrima while he eulogized about the Dutch countryside in his pedantic, precise English, and indeed it looked delightful under the light blue sky, even though the sunshine was pale and without warmth.

Friso's house, when they reached it, looked superb against its calm background, and her welcome was everything that could have been desired. Cressida bade Doctor Herrima goodbye and went indoors with Harriet to drink coffee and play with the babies until Friso came home for lunch, a delightful domestic meal which left her full of vague feelings of loneliness and longing for a home and a family of her own. Perhaps, she thought forlornly, they were made worse because she loved Giles. She shook the thought from her, for little Friso was demanding her attention.

It was impossible to feel unhappy for long in that happy household, though; and although she hadn't told Harriet about her parents' deaths she seemed to know all about it and what was more, talked about them in a perfectly natural way, asking Cressida about her home, giving her a chance to talk about them, something she knew now she had been longing to do for weeks. By tea-time she was laughing and talking as though she hadn't a care in the world, and as she helped put the babies to bed she said rather shyly, 'I feel quite different, Harry—talking about Mother and Father ... I suppose I've had it all bottled up inside me. And being here with you—you're so happy.'

Her youthful hostess gave her a shrewd look. 'Yes, we are,' she said simply. 'I never knew that I could be so happy.' She smiled to herself. 'Friso and I— when we first met, you know—we weren't friends at first—at least I wasn't, and I thought he was going to marry someone else. He's like a rock, Cressida. You'll meet someone like him one day.'

It would have been lovely to confide to Harry that she already knew her particular rock and a lot of good it had done her. She managed some laughing reply and went with her hostess to tidy herself for dinner. Told to make her own way down to the drawing-room when she was ready, she made leisurely repairs to her face and hair, and went back downstairs.

The drawing-room appeared empty as she entered it; she was making her way down to the welcome warmth of the great fire at the opposite end of the room when Giles got out of a great winged chair turned a little away from her and she stopped short, said 'Oh ...' and waited for her breath to come back.

'Now that is the kind of enthusiastic welcome I like,' he observed blandly.

'You surprised me.'

'Oh, dear—like meeting a bull in a field or finding a spider in the bed?'

Cressida chuckled despite herself. 'Don't be absurd—I just didn't expect to see you.'

He had drawn up a small crinoline chair to the fire for her and then sat down opposite her. 'I've been invited to dinner,' he told her, 'so I'll drive you back.'

'Well— thank you; Friso was going to ...'

'Friso has a wife and three children he adores and never sees enough of; if you could steel yourself to endure my company instead of his, I fancy he will be secretly delighted; he treasures his evenings at home with Harry.'

Cressida said 'Oh,' again, and Giles laughed and got up as Harriet and Friso came in. The talk became general at once and stayed that way while they had their drinks and went in to dinner, and afterwards they sat round the fire, drinking their coffee; the two girls together talking about clothes and babies, and the two men, wreathed in cigar smoke, discussing some knotty medical problem in their own tongue.

'I suppose you speak perfect Dutch,' observed Cressida enviously.

Harriet laughed. 'Me? Heavens, no—Friso and I always speak English when we're together. I speak Dutch to Anna and Hans and our Dutch friends, of course, and I get along well enough in the shops. I had lessons for a year, but I'm by no means perfect.' She smiled. 'I don't suppose you've needed to speak Dutch, have you, though it must have been awkward when you all had the 'flu.'

'It was, but Juffrouw Naald and I have invented our own way of talking to each other; it works very well.' Cressida paused as the dainty little Sèvres clock on the table beside them chimed the hour. 'It's nine o'clock—shouldn't we be going? I've been here almost all day.'

Harriet laughed. 'And very nice too—you simply must come again before you go back to England. Giles comes quite often, you could come with him.' Something in Cressida's face made her add: 'Or Friso could pick you up when he goes to Groningen —he has some beds at the hospital there.'

They left half an hour later, and Cressida, looking back as they went down the short drive, saw that the great front door was still open and Friso

124

and Harriet were standing just inside, arm-in-arm with the dogs sitting in a tight bunch beside them. She spoke her thoughts aloud. 'They're very happy, aren't they?'

Giles turned the car into the narrow road. 'Very. Wasn't it your Jane Austen who wrote "Happiness in marriage is entirely a matter of chance"? I don't agree with her—do you, Cressida?'

'I don't know,' she sad soberly. 'I've not been married, so how would I be able to tell?'

It was a dark night now with a fitful moon fighting to escape the clouds which threatened to engulf it; it was cold too, she could see the frost sparkling in the fields and the thin ice already covering the canals. They were almost at their journey's end, driving along a dyke with a canal on either side, when the Bentley's powerful headlamps pinpointed a car ahead of them. It was being driven slowly, weaving from one side of the road to the other, and Cressida could see frightened faces looking at them from the rear window.

The doctor had slowed down. 'Steering gone?' he wondered out loud. 'A drunk? A coronary perhaps —he'll be in the canal if he doesn't watch out.'

He was proved right almost immediately—the car in front of them slewed across the road and toppled quite slowly into the canal. Giles slammed on the brakes and was out of the car almost before the other vehicle had hit the water.

Cressida gave a gasp of horror and got out too. She had no idea how one set about getting out the occupants of a drowning car, especially on a dark, bitter cold night. A torch, she thought wildly as she scrambled on to the slippery grass, but the doctor already had one in his hand; he thrust it at her and peeled off his coat, elegant jacket and waistcoat and dumped them on the grass.

'There were children, I think—I'll get them first,' he told her with a calmness she envied. 'You may have to take them from me—better get your coat off, no point in getting it wet.'

He took the torch from her and set it on the ground where its beam would give them some light, then slid into the black, icy water. Cressida watched him disappear with even greater horror and then floundered down the bank herself, clutching frantically at the rough, slippery grass as she tried to find a firm foothold; she was petrified by now, but the occupants of the car would be even more so; besides, Giles was there ... She dipped a cautious booted foot into the water, and then another, and discovered, a little late in the day, that the bank was sheer, there was no ground under her feet ... She was still clinging to the grass with both hands, her legs getting more and more numb with every second, when there was an oily splash close to her and the doctor's powerful frame, covered in mud and weed, appeared. He had a small child across his shoulder; he thrust him at her without a word and disappeared into the murky depths again.

Cressida had had to let go of her grass; now she bobbed up and down with the limp little creature held awkwardly to her, but a mouthful of muddy water galvanised her into action; somehow she scrambled up the bank and laid the child down. There was no time to examine him; she rolled him on to his stomach, turned the wet head carefully to one side and slid, very reluctantly, back into the canal.

Just in time; the doctor surfaced almost beside her, pushed a slightly older child towards her, said: 'There's a woman—the man's dead,' and slid silently back. Cressida was getting over her fright now; the child was a good deal heavier than the first one, but what could be done once would be done again. She clawed her precarious way on to the bank once more, half drowning both herself and the child, and laid it beside the other little form. She was numb with cold by now and her boots—the only good boots she had, too—were filled with water and like lead on her feet, and her clothes clung wetly, turned icy in the wind. The only thing which wasn't quite ruined was her fur cap, and if the doctor expected her to haul a grown woman on to the bank, that would be a ruin too.

But he didn't; he heaved a young, stoutly built woman out of the water himself, and when she made feeble attempts to help herself, told Cressida to get her higher up the bank before he ducked back into the water again.

It was a struggle, for Cressida didn't know enough Dutch to encourage her half-drowned companion, or tell her what to do; she caught a handful of coat across the woman's back and heaved and tugged and then pushed from behind, until the pair of them were lying by the children.

'Shan't be a minute,' Cressida told the woman, quite uselessly, and went slithering down the bank for the last time.

Giles was having no easy task; the man was short but heavily built and a dead weight. He pushed him out of the water and told Cressida to hang on to his shoulders while he got himself out. But he wouldn't let her help after that, but hauled the man up the bank to where the others lay. Cressida, eager to join him, got to her feet, forgetting that they were numbed to deadness by now. Her first step sent her slithering down the bank and into the water once again, a good deal faster this time, so that she went under and came up with a terrified yelp which brought the doctor into the canal beside her.

'Good God girl,' he snapped, 'did you have to fall in too? And it's only a couple of feet from the bank.'

In the torch's light, she could see how white and haggard his face was, and he was in a rage with her, too.

She steadied her chattering teeth to tell him, 'I can't swim.'

CHAPTER SEVEN

IF Cressida hadn't been soaking wet and almost dead with cold and fright, the consternation on Giles' face might have given her enormous pleasure. As it was, she clutched his shirt sleeves with terrified fingers and kept her eyes shut. And when he spoke, it was in his own language; it sounded very forceful, and probably he was as angry as he looked. She opened one eye to see, and he looked so ferocious that she shut it again as she was tossed, without much respect for her person, on to the bank. 'Get into the car,' he ordered her in a no-nonsense voice, 'the front seat. You can take the smallest child on your lap, the others can go in the back.'

She stumbled painfully up the bank and he put out an arm and hauled her along beside him. 'But the man,' she protested weakly, 'he's ...'

'Yes, he is, but we must still get to hospital with all despatch. Luckily, the others are in no fit state to realise ...'

The child he put into her lap was breathing, and despite the cold and wet, a little colour was creeping into his cheeks; Cressida had barely made sure of that before the doctor had got the other three into the back of the car and had climbed in beside her, throwing her coat and his behind him.

'Thank heaven they didn't have time to drown—

they're shocked and they've taken in a lot of water, but bar accidents, they should be all right, excepting for the man, of course—poor fellow.' He started the car, dripping muddy water over everything, and said with deliberate cheerfulness. 'Lord, how we do smell!'

His remark recalled her to her own slimy, weedy condition. Perhaps, when the poor souls with them had been taken care of, she might be allowed to take a bath and borrow some dry clothes at the hospital, but there was no point in worrying about that at the moment; she began to rub the small icy hands and feet as best she might, for the doctor was driving at speed.

'Which hospital?' she asked.

'Groningen. We're on a country road which will bring us out at Kollum. I had intended to go across country from there, but now we can take the other fork and join the motorway—it's only another few minutes now.' He added, 'I can get along faster.'

Cressida received this information with no enthusiasm at all; true, the sooner they got to the hospital, the better, but she was in no state to travel at a hundred miles an hour or more; they were already doing eighty on a road intended for sedate local traffic. She forced her eyes from the speedometer and bent her attention on to the child. When she looked up presently she saw the flashing blue lamp ahead of them and gasped: 'A police car, and heaven knows what speed you're doing ...'

'A hundred and ten miles an hour,' stated the doctor placidly, 'and they're just the people we want.' He sent the Bentley roaring ahead, to draw up alongside the police car, open his window and shout across to its driver. Both cars pulled up then and one of the policemen got out, took a look in the car, listened to what the doctor had to say, nodded, got back into his own car and rocketed ahead, siren blaring, blue light flashing. the Bentley hard on his bumper.

It was like being in a particularly nasty dream, thought Cressida muzzily. She was feeling sick now and very woried about the child on her lap; his breathing had become loud and rasping and his pulse was rising.

'Is it far?' she asked.

'Child not too good? At this rate, less than five minutes. Do you want me to stop?'

'No—there's nothing much we can do, is there, and the others need attention as quickly as possible.'

The car's blessed warmth was beginning to creep into her bones. Her teeth had stopped chattering too, although water was trickling down her back, accumulating in icy patches here and there. She sighed with relief when the first houses of Groningen closed in around them. They hardly slackened their pace going through the city: the police car, still ahead, carved a way for them through the scanty traffic and pulled up at last in the hospital's forecourt.

The police must have radioed ahead, for there was another police car waiting and a group of doctors, nurses and porters poised ready with their trolleys. Giles got out of the car, said: 'Stay there,' to Cressida and went to give brief instructions to those waiting. She watched the brisk transport of the unfortunate occupants of the car, sitting in her sopping, ruined clothes—at least the mother and two children were alive; the children crying thinly, the mother tearful too and not yet completely conscious. Giles had his head through the police car window now, talking to its occupants, and then he was beside her again, and the car purred into life. She thought he said: 'Poor little Cressida,' but she was so weary and bemused that she decided that she had fancied it. She was too tired even to ask where they were going.

Not very far, it seemed—across the city and into a tree-lined street with a canal running down its centre. The houses on either side were mostly in darkness, but she caught glimpses of them in the car's headlamps; great gabled mansions standing shoulder to shoulder, their fronts richly decorated with carved wreaths of flowers, their splendid windows guarded by shutters. The doctor stopped the car in front of one of these and got out, to carry her across the narrow brick pavement and up double steps to a massive carved door which someone was holding open. She heard a man's voice answering the doctor when he spoke, and the sound of a dog's heavy breathing as she was borne rapidly along a narrow hallway into an inner hall and then up a staircase set at right angles to it. There was someone else with them now, hurrying just in front, making soothing sounds, and at the top of the staircase, crossing the gallery to open a door for them.

She felt herself laid down on a bed and for a moment Giles's face was bent over hers. He still looked very white and angry. Cressida closed her eyes and sighed. His anger was something she couldn't cope with just then, all she wanted to do was to be allowed to sleep; she was long past caring about her wet, cold clothes and her numb feet.

'No, you don't,' said the doctor, 'not yet. Ineke here will help you undress and into a hot bath, then you are to have a warm drink and be allowed to sleep for as long as you like.'

'Doctor van Blom . . .?' she asked sleepily.

'I'll telephone him now.'

'You'll catch your death of cold,' she told him owlishly, and heard him laugh.

'Here's Ineke,' he said, and went away.

Ineke was plump and middle-aged, with a kind, plain face and small, twinkling boot-button eyes. She clucked and soothed as she peeled off Cressida's wet things, wrapped her in an enormous bath towel and led her to the bathroom adjoining, where she soaked in the fragrant hot water while Ineke washed her filthy hair. She would have stayed to fall asleep if she hadn't been firmly helped out, dried, put into a voluminous, long-sleeved, high-necked nightgown of finest silk and put back to bed where her kindly helper dried her hair, saw that she drank the milk which had been set ready by her bed, and finally, with another flow of clucks and tuts, allowed her to lie down and close her eyes. Cressida was aware that she was being tucked in before she slept.

She awoke to a fairytale room. She sat up in bed,

feeling little the worse for her ducking, and looked around her. It was a pretty apartment, the furniture of satinwood polished to glowing brilliance, the curtains and bedspread and chair covers in pale chintzes of pinks and blues. The bed was elaborately carved at head and foot and covered with a thick pink eiderdown, and the sheets, she noticed with some awe, were very fine linen, embroidered and edged with lace. She sat up a little higher in bed as she counted the hours rung out by the various churches in the neighbourhood—ten o'clock; she would have to get up, but a glance round the room revealed the fact that none of her clothes were visible. She would have to find someone . . .

She had one foot out of bed when there was a knock on the door and she put it back in again and called 'Come in'. Giles entered, looking immaculate, well rested and not in the least like a man who had spent quite a few minutes in an icy canal only a few hours earlier. There was a dog with him, an Irish wolfhound, looking at her with a benevolent, whiskered face. His hullo was casual and followed by his amused: 'Good lord, you're lost in that thing, aren't you?'

Cressida regarded the generous folds of silk with pleasure. 'It's pure silk,' she told him with satisfaction, 'and the lace is handmade, I think—quite beautiful.'

He smiled and came to sit on the edge of the bed. 'Feeling better?'

'Yes, thank you. I had a lovely sleep. Do you feel all right?'

His careless 'Of course,' made her feel foolish for asking, so that her next question was abrupt. 'Where am I?'

'Ah, the classic remark of all heroines. You're in my house.'

'Oh, and don't call me a heroine—I let you down dreadfully.'

He got up from the bed and went to look out of the window. 'You were a very brave girl—it needed courage to do what you did.'

Before she could stop herself, she said: 'But you were there . . .' He gave her a long, thoughtful look and she added hastily: 'What I mean is—well . . .' It was impossible to say what she meant; that because he had been there, she had felt quite sure that he would save her if she needed saving; that her trust had been greater than her fear. She stared at him silently and then when he smiled slowly, looked away and said in a high voice: 'What a gorgeous dog,' and then: 'It's very late. I hope I haven't disorganised your household. If I could have my clothes I'll dress, then I could perhaps telephone Doctor van Blom.'

'I have already done so; I told him that I would bring you back after lunch. Ineke is seeing to your clothes, I believe, and she will be here with your breakfast in a few minutes. I'm on my way to my consulting rooms and I'll be back to pick you up just after one o'clock. Ineke will see about your lunch.' As he spoke the housekeeper came in with a tray. 'I'll leave you to enjoy your breakfast.'

He was as good as his word. It had barely chimed

the hour when he entered the house once more, and Cressida, once more in her own clothes, neatly cleaned and pressed but ruined for all that, was drinking her second cup of coffee after her lunch. She had spent an interesting morning, going downstairs rather hesitantly after she had bathed and dressed, to find a rotund little man with a merry face hovering in the hall. His 'Good morning, Miss Bingley,' took her by surprise, but she wished him a good morning too and gave him an inquiring look.

'I am Doctor van der Teile's houseman, Beeker, miss,' he informed her in heavily accented English. 'I opened the door to you last night, but you were too tired to notice anyone.' He waved a hand across the hall. 'If you would like to sit in this room? We call it the small parlour; the doctor spends a good deal of his time here—and in his study, of course. The other reception rooms are rather large and used only for company.'

He opened a double door and ushered her into a fair-sized room, most comfortably furnished with a well-balanced arrangement of beautiful old furniture and easy chairs. There were two velvet-covered sofas, one each side of the fireplace, and a smaller chair had been drawn up to the bright fire burning in it. 'I think you will find this a comfortable seat,' said Beeker in a kindly voice. 'You will find the English papers on a small table beside you. Ineke will be in at once with your coffee, miss.'

He beamed at her and trotted away and the housekeeper swept in with the coffee tray and the dog at her heels. She fussed gently around in a fashion which Cressida found quite delightful and presently went away, leaving her to read the papers and drink her coffee, while Barker, the dog, stretched himself before the fire and kept her company. Beeker had come back several times during the morning, to make up the fire in the marble hearth, to inquire if she would like more coffee; at what time she would like lunch; if she had sufficient to read ... she had thought that in this day and age, there were no longer people like Beeker and Incke, lapping one around with every comfort and seeming to enjoy it.

At lunch-time, when Beeker came to fetch her, explaining that they had laid the table in the small dining-room for her—'the large dining-room seats sixteen persons,' he explained further—she ventured to ask him how long he had been with the doctor.

'Oh, before he was born, miss—I came as a house-boy to the doctor's father. Incke has been here almost as long. Of course there are two young girls who help in the house.'

He ushered her into a room across the hall, a small, panelled apartment with a rich, many-coloured carpet and sapphire blue brocade curtains at its tall, narrow windows. The dining table was circular, of inlaid walnut, as were the four chairs placed round it. Cressida ran her fingers lovingly over the marquetry as she sat down, and looked appreciatively at the fine napery and silver before her; Giles lived in some style, he must have an enormous and very lucrative practice. She frowned faintly; it would have been nice to have known all about him, but pointless, too.

Beeker stayed in the room while she ate: soup, a little vol-au-vent as light as air, filled with prawns, cold meat, a delicious salad and a variety of breads and excellent coffee with it. It was he who mentioned their watery adventure of the previous evening. 'Very brave of you, Miss Bingley, if I may say so. Ineke thinks so too. Our canals can be very unpleasant even for those who can swim. We are sorry that your clothes are spoiled, although we have done our best.'

'You've both been super,' declared Cressida. 'I thought they were a write-off—er—useless, but at least I can wear them back. I'm sorry you've had so much extra work because of me.'

Beeker smiled all over his face. 'A pleasure, miss. I think the doctor has just entered the house.'

Giles came in a moment later and Cressida made haste to say: 'I'm sorry I forgot to ask after those poor people—are they all right?'

'They are doing very well. The little boy may have to stay in for a time, but his mother and the other child will go home in a day or so.'

He had thrown off his coat and was rubbing Barker's ears, and as Beeker came back with a tray of coffee, he sat himself down in a winged armchair by the fire.

'And your mother? I did mean to ask after her too ...'

'She is doing very well—I've just been with her. She sends her love to you.'

Cressida digested this in silence; perhaps he was just being kind, for somehow his forthright parent didn't seem the kind of person to send her love indiscriminately.

'No, I didn't make that up,' said the doctor quickly. 'She likes you.'

She went a little pink. 'I like her too.'

'Good, you cannot imagine what a relief that is to me.' He was laughing at her and she had no idea why, so she asked, to be told: 'Oh, we'll go into that some other time. If you're ready, we'll go—I've one or two patients to see and I want to have a look at Doctor van Blom at the same time.'

Cressida went straight back to her typing as soon as they arrived, despite Doctor van Blom's protests. 'I only got wet,' she told him, 'and honestly, I feel fine.'

So she retired to the study and got out the manuscript and went to work on it at once—she was almost at the end now; another few days—a week perhaps, and she would be finished and getting ready to go back home to Aunt Emily and the tiresome job of looking for a new post. She paused in her work to think about it and became so gloomy that she gave it up presently and went back to her typing.

Juffrouw Naald brought her her tea. The doctors, she made Cressida understand, were in consultation and did not wish to be disturbed, and towards the end of the afternoon she heard the front door close

139

and the Bentley's gentle, almost soundless engine start up. Giles had gone; he could at least have put his head round the door and wished her goodbye. What a waste of time it was, she thought crossly, loving someone who treated her in such an offhand fashion—although he had no reason to do otherwise, especially when he was about to marry Monique de Vries. Cressida took out her ill feeling on the typewriter so that it jammed and she was forced to spend the rest of the evening getting it to go again.

It was the next morning, as she settled down to work after breakfast, that Giles walked in. She wished him good morning in a surprised voice and asked: 'Shall I fetch Doctor van Blom, or was it Doctor Herrima you wanted?'

'Neither. I came to see you, Cressida.'

'Me? Whatever for?'

He sat down in his partner's chair behind the desk. 'Will you marry me?'

The sheet of paper she was holding fluttered to the ground. When she found her voice she repeated 'Marry you?' in an unbelieving kind of way, and then: 'But you're going to marry Mevrouw de Vries.'

If he was surprised he didn't show it but replied blandly: 'Am I? Whoever told you that? I'm not, you know. She's in Paris now and is getting married there today.'

Something in his voice made her ask: 'Didn't you know that she was going to marry?'

'Not until this morning.'

Cressida's hands were clenched tightly in her lap, rage bubbled up so fiercely inside her that she could barely utter. 'And so you came straight here and asked me to marry you!' Her voice was a trifle loud, and despite her efforts, shook a little. 'Charming—on the rebound, I presume.'

There was no expression on his face, only his eyes had become so cold that she shivered. 'Is that what you think? That I wanted Monique and because I couldn't have her, I decided to ask the first girl I saw to marry me in her place?' His voice was unhurried and silky and although he was smiling now, she wished he wouldn't.

She looked at her tightly entwined hands. 'What else am I to think? I can hardly suppose that you love me—I may be a fool, but not such a fool as all that! Why, you don't even like me, you get furious with me for no reason at all ... the other night, in that beastly canal you you shouted at me because I fell in, and you didn't mind at all when I didn't get any supper, and when you were here it was: "Cressida, get up, Cressida, go to bed, Cressida, help in the surgery, Cressida, drive the Bentley" ... and now here you are ...' her voice rose with the strength of her feelings, 'asking me to marry you!'

The doctor had been watching her closely during her tirade. Now when he spoke his voice was quite different; kind and gentle and understanding. 'I've taken you by surprise, and you are quite right, I have never given you any reason to believe that I loved you and now I have been clumsy—I'll say none of the things I intended to say, for I don't think it would help at all, but I had thought—I had hoped ...' he paused to smile at her. 'Go back to England and think about it and make up your mind there, and in the meantime, don't stop me from seeing as much of you as I possibly can.'

He came round the desk and pulled her to her feet. 'I think we might be very happy together,' he said, and kissed her—a very gentle kiss. Illogically, she would have liked to have been swept off her feet and kissed breathless, whether he meant it or not ...

'I'm free until this evening.' He spoke casually, as though none of their astonishing conversation had taken place. 'Shall we go somewhere for lunch? Hilversum, perhaps? I feel like a long drive. I promise you I won't talk about us at all, not unless you want it.'

'But haven't you any patients?' she asked doubtfully.

'Not today.' He smiled at her, crossed the room and covered her typewriter. 'You look pale, dear girl, you need a change of scene.'

She needed more than that; she needed several hours alone somewhere, so that she could think, but she could see that she wasn't going to get them at present. Besides, she knew that she would go with him; he was restless and probably dreadfully unhappy, for he hadn't denied that he loved Monique. Her marriage must have come as a dreadful shock to him. Cressida remembered how close they had been standing that time she had gone down for something to eat; he must have felt quite sure of her then, and now the bottom had tumbled out of his world. It seemed likely that he hadn't meant a word of his amazing proposal; shock did strange things to people, but loving him as she did, she could help him in the only way possible; spending the next few hours with him, helping him to pass the time until his first shock and anger were spent.

She said quietly: 'I'll get my coat, I'd like a long drive too.' She paused at the door. 'I'll tell Doctor van Blom—you don't think he'll mind?'

'No, for I've already asked him. He's been worrying about you working too hard, but he's in his surgery if you want him.'

She peered round the door on her way upstairs and his round, cheerful face lit up when he saw her. 'Now I am content,' he declared. 'You will have a day's holiday and be happy—and make Giles happy too.'

So he too knew about Monique. Cressida said soberly, 'I'll try.'

And she did, keeping up a cheerful flow of chat throughout their long drive, although her companion contributed very little in reply, only brief answers or an occasional grunt, but she persevered, ignoring his preoccupied manner and stern profile.

She kept it up throughout their lunch in the splendid hotel in Hilversum to which he took her, pretending a great interest in the food and trying not to notice his own lack of appetite, and after their meal, when he took her walking in the town, she offered intelligent comments and asked questions which he was forced to exert himself to answer.

143

She had a headache by this time, and heartache too; perhaps it had been a mistake to go with him, perhaps he would have been better off with his own thoughts, however bitter. But apparently not; they were almost back at Augustinusga when he said warmly: 'Thank you, Cressida—you've helped me through the day and you haven't asked a single question—not even looked curious. I only wish we could spend the evening together, but it's my night for the clinic.'

'I'll come with you,' she said instantly, 'if you'll have me. There must be something I can do there, and as you'll have to drive me back afterwards you'll be so tired, you'll sleep.' She added carefully: 'But only if you like the idea.'

'I would like it, very much. The clinic finishes about nine o'clock, we'll go somewhere and have a meal before I drive you back,' and when she objected: 'That will tire me out even better.'

Someone found her an overall at the clinic and she was given the task of helping the elderly patients off with their coats and scarves and woollies and then getting them back into them again when the doctor had finished with them. It was a pleasant surprise to discover that she needed no knowledge of Dutch for this simple task; nods and smiles and encouraging murmurs were quite sufficient to promote understanding. True, several of the smaller patients burst into tears for one reason or another, but she discovered that as long as she spoke to them soothingly it really didn't seem to matter that they couldn't understand a word of what she was saying.

The evening passed quickly, even with the two nurses on duty; they all had their work cut out, what with ushering patients back and forth, collecting notes, finding X-rays, sending the patients on their way again and tidying up when there was a moment to spare.

Cressida saw very little of the doctor; a brief glimpse of him sitting at his desk as she admitted or removed a patient; withdrawn, totally engrossed in his work, quite remote from the man who had asked her, so surprisingly, to marry him. It might be a good thing to forget that, she decided, as she swathed a dear old man in a succession of winter garments. She had had several proposals in the last few years, but never one quite as strange as this one, and all the more strange because he didn't strike her as an impulsive man at all. But it must have been impulse which had caused him to speak as he had.

She saw the last patient off the premises and went to help the nurses with the clearing up; at least the day was almost over; she wasn't certain about his invitation to supper and perhaps it would be as well not to mention it. But he did, coming out of his surgery as she was washing down the tables and rearranging the magazines.

'*Erwten* soup,' he observed, 'with french bread and lots of butter and cups of coffee—there's a small snack bar near here, will that suit you?'

It suited her very well; they walked the short distance together talking about the clinic, Giles going over some cases in his deliberate way, weighing the pros and cons, assessing their chances of improvement, mulling over the cases which might need surgery later on. Cressida listened carefully, encouraging him to talk, treasuring the thought that he confided in her, just as though she were an old trusted friend or someone close—his wife. She wondered if he had talked to Monique in this fashion and thought it unlikely, but there was no way of finding out. However, he hadn't mentioned her again and she felt sure that he wasn't going to.

They reached the snack bar and took a small table in its window, where they had their pea soup and drank several cups of coffee, talking now of his mother, his partners' practice, the 'flu epidemic, which had, mercifully lost its grip, and the chances of a cold winter ahead. The kind of talk between friends, she was beginning to hope.

They drove back in silence, but it was a friendly silence, and when they reached his partners' house, Giles went with her to the door and unlocked it with his key and went into the hall with her, where they met Juffrouw Naald, who smiled with pleasure at the sight of them and went at once to fetch coffee. They had it in the sitting-room, which was warm and smelled of cigars. Cressida, worn out with the effort she had been making all day, felt comfortably drowsy.

'You're tired, aren't you?' asked Giles. 'Go to bed, I'll see myself out.'

'Well, I'll pour some more coffee first,' said Cressida, anxious to spin out the time spent in his company as long as possible. 'I enjoyed the day very much—Hilversum was very interesting, I had no idea ...' She caught his eye and stopped because he was smiling.

'It's all right,' he told her, 'my rage has blown itself out, you don't have to distract my thoughts any more.' He took the cup she was offering him. 'Mama is coming out of hospital tomorrow. Will you come with me to fetch her home?'

'I'd like to, if Doctor van Blom doesn't mind.'

'It won't be until after six o'clock—I've too much to do. She will be staying with me for a week or two, just until she is quite fit.'

'Oh, I thought she lived with you.'

'She has a house just outside Groningen—a small villa my father bought for her a long time ago. She lives there most of the time, although she spends the odd week or so with me.' He got to his feet and crossed the room to pull her gently from her chair.

'How much more work have you to do on that book?' he wanted to know quietly.

'I'm on the last chapter—I've done most of the cross-references as I went along, so I only have the final correcting to do then. About three days.'

If she had hoped that he would refer to the future, she was to be disappointed. He merely re-iterated: 'Go to bed, Cressida,' and walked her to the door. He made no attempt to kiss her good-night; she went quickly upstairs, torn between regret that he hadn't and peevishness that he had, apparently, not wanted to.

She worked hard throughout the next day, with a half-formed idea at the back of her mind that it

147

would serve him right if she finished her job earlier than she had told him, and then slipped away without saying anything to him—it wasn't what she wanted to do, of course; it would be a mean trick to play, but on the other hand there was absolutely no reason why she shouldn't do what she pleased—Giles had taken her a little for granted, she told herself indignantly.

She became increasingly peevish as the day wore on, so that by the time he arrived that evening her greeting was cold and very offhand, and when he inquired after her progress, answered him so evasively that he lifted an eyebrow at her and asked her affably enough if she was feeling quite well.

'I have never felt better,' she assured him snappily, and went to get her coat.

It seemed he hadn't noticed her ill-humour, for he kept up a cheerful flow of remarks as they drove to Groningen. But when they were on their way to his mother's room and she stole a look at him, she saw that something was worrying him still; there was a faint frown between his thick brows and his mouth was grim. But when they reached the invalid's room, there was neither frown nor grimness. He supervised his parent's departure with good-humoured patience, helped her carefully into the Bentley, invited Cressida to sit in the back of the car, and drove to his home.

Beeker was hovering, ready to open the door when they arrived, and Ineke was there too, so were the two girls who helped in the house; Mevrouw van der Teile was welcomed like royalty, and responded with all the graciousness of such. Cressida, bearing a variety of rugs, shawls, and flowers which at the last moment the patient felt she could not leave behind, was a little amused by it all, but she was touched, too, that Giles' mother should be greeted with such pleasure and affection, despite her imperious manner. She was borne upstairs, with Cressida still trailing behind, while the doctor went to his study to attend to some urgent telephone message. She was got to bed, the flowers arranged exactly as she wished, the bedjacket she fancied found and put on, her hair rearranged, and finally, a dainty tray with a light supper brought in.

Cressida, with nothing to do for the moment, leaned over the end of the wide canopied bed and surveyed its occupant, who was nibbling at the creamed chicken Ineke had prepared for her.

'I am a tiresome old lady, am I not?' asked Mevrouw van der Teile suddenly, and bit with appetite into a finger of toast.

'No,' said Cressida, 'for you're not old and you're not tiresome. I was just thinking, how delightful to be held in such affection—not just by Giles, but by everyone here.'

'Yes, it is, isn't it?' agreed her companion with some complacency, then said so sharply that Cressida jumped, 'Giles is upset and very angry. You know why?'

'Yes.'

'I expected better of Monique de Vries; the least that can be said is that it was unkind and wrong not to tell him.' She gave a dignified snort. 'Going to Paris to buy clothes—she told us all—and then breaking her word to him!'

Cressida wandered away to a corner of the room where the light was dim. 'I expect he'll get over it,' she suggested, and made great work of studying a charming little flower painting on the wall.

'Oh, yes, of course he will—but men remember that sort of thing. I've said nothing, of course. When he wants to, he'll no doubt tell me everything there is to know.'

Cressida murmured something and wished very much for the conversation to end. She had her wish, for the doctor came in at that moment, spent a few minutes talking to his mother and then announced that dinner was awaiting them downstairs.

Cressida hadn't expected that; she had thrown off her coat when she had come into the house, and flung the no longer new fur cap after it, and she wasn't as tidy as usual. 'My hair——' she began, and was interrupted by his impatient: 'It looks perfectly all right to me, but if it's going to spoil your dinner, Ineke shall take you somewhere and you can do whatever it is needs doing.'

'Of course Cressida wishes to freshen up,' declared his mother severely. 'Ring the bell for Ineke, Giles, and you may stay with me for a few moments while she is doing it.'

Cressida was taken to the room she had occupied previously, and presently, very neat once more, went down to the sitting-room where Giles was waiting to give her a drink before ushering her into the dining-room. There Beeker, looking jollier than ever, served them with iced melon, lobster Thermidor, and a strawberry shortcake, made, she discovered, with fresh strawberries. She turned surprised eyes upon her host, who smiled blandly across the table at her and said:

'Shocked, Cressida? Appalled at the wicked extravagance of fresh strawberries in December? Perhaps you will enjoy them better if I tell you that they're grown at a small farm I own in Limburg— it has some rather fine hothouses there and a very old gardener who can grow anything. You shall meet him one day.'

It seemed prudent to let that pass; she made some trivial remark about Limburg, and he followed her lead, his eyes twinkling.

Cressida went to say goodnight to Mevrouw van der Teile after they had had their coffee in the sitting-room, and not much later, Giles drove her back to Augustinusga. When they arrived he got out of the car and opened the house door for her, but he didn't come in. But this time he did kiss her with fierce urgency, and then without a word pushed her gently through the door and closed it between them, leaving her to stand in the dim hall, wondering how anyone with a heart as broken as his could kiss like that. Probably, she thought wistfully, he had been pretending that she was Monique.

CHAPTER EIGHT

Two days later Cressida had the manuscript finished, corrected and on Doctor van Blom's desk for his scrutiny. She had seen nothing of Giles and when she had asked Doctor Herrima at dinner that evening, in a studiedly nonchalant voice, if his partner had gone away, he had looked at her in some surprise and said no, he had been on the telephone not an hour since, and then he had been at his consulting rooms.

Cressida had at once plunged into conversation about something quite different and they had all had a second glass of the champagne Doctor van Blom had produced in honour of the completion of his book. Giles wasn't mentioned again, and she went to bed in quite a nasty temper, although she concealed that fact from her elderly companions.

The next morning, after a wakeful night, she broached the subject of her leaving. They were sitting at breakfast, and two pairs of eyes regarded her with consternation. 'My dear Cressida,' said Doctor van Blom, 'you surely can't mean to leave us so suddenly? I know that my book is finished, but could you not stay for a day or so longer? You have no job waiting for you?'

She had to admit that she hadn't, and she was mustering several good reasons why she should return to England as soon as possible when the reason for her desire to be gone entered the room, closely followed by Juffrouw Naald, bearing fresh coffee.

'Cressida feels that she should leave us at once,' stated Doctor van Blom instantly.

Giles seated himself at the table and stared across it at her as she poured his coffee. 'Does she indeed? Now, I wonder why.'

'I have to get another job,' she told him, a little too quickly.

He brushed that aside. 'Have you made your decision?' he asked, and smiled a little although his eyes were intent on her, and she met them unflinchingly although she had gone pink.

'No,' she said, 'I haven't.'

He nodded. 'So you wish to go back to England—you want time.'

It was silly to say that; she didn't want time; here she was, ready and waiting to fling herself into his arms, only how could she with Monique's lovely shadow between them? She said: 'Yes, I do. I think we both do.'

He smiled a little. 'I can't agree with you there, but I'll not hurry you—I've already told you that.'

She said slowly, 'Yes, I know.' She had quite forgotten their two companions, sitting like two elderly mice, drinking in every word. 'You see, Giles, I have to be sure.' She didn't explain that it was of him she had to be sure. If he had said, just once, that he loved her, she wouldn't have hesitated, but he hadn't—probably by now he was regretting his impulsiveness; she would have to give him the opportunity of backing out, and that could be done more easily once she was miles away from him.

'When do you want to go?' he asked casually.

'Well, soon. It's too late to go tomorrow, isn't it, but the day after that?' She remembered the two silent doctors then. 'You wouldn't mind? I've loved being here with you, but I think it would be best if I went home as quickly as possible.'

'I've asked Cressida to marry me,' Giles spoke quietly, 'and for some reason she doesn't take me seriously.' He grinned suddenly at her across the table and went on with uncanny insight: 'She thinks that if she is in England and I'm here, we can jilt each other more easily.'

It was disconcerting to have her thoughts read so accurately. She felt the colour come into her face and was furious with herself for it, especially as all three men were looking at her. It was Doctor Herrima who said: 'How refreshing to see a girl blush —they never do these days. Do please take Giles seriously, Cressida, it would make us both very happy.' He chuckled. 'Besides, it would keep you in the practice, wouldn't it?'

He laughed comfortably at his little joke and his partner with him. Giles laughed too, only there was mockery in it, as though he knew exactly what she was thinking. She hoped he didn't, and said rather coldly, because the smile had annoyed her: 'I could take your manuscript with me, Doctor van Blom— it's expected on the twelfth, isn't it? If I travel the day after tomorrow, I could take it to the publishers, it's quicker and safer than the post.'

'Going home to Aunt Emily?' asked Giles carelessly.

She had told him about her aunt, she had even described exactly where she lived. 'Yes,' and then she added hastily: 'I shall probably get another job right away, though—I might just as well call in at the agency while I'm in London.'

'A splendid idea,' observed Giles genially. 'Well, we shall all be sorry to see you go, Cressida. I'm going back to Groningen very shortly. How about coming back with me and saying goodbye to Mama? And surely you want to do some shopping ...'

True, she did, and she couldn't go without saying goodbye to Mevrouw van der Teile. She agreed a little ungraciously, because he had trapped her into it, excused herself with the plea that she had the typewriter to clean, and left the three men still sitting round the breakfast table, although they wouldn't be there long; surgery was almost due to start.

She went into the study and sat down at the desk; she would clean the typewriter another time, she decided; she could better employ her time in making up her mind as to her future. She supposed that if she hadn't loved Giles so very much, she might have accepted him; but to marry him now, feeling as she did about him, would spell disaster; she would never know how much he loved Monique, or what his real feelings for herself were; a man could marry for a variety of reasons, not necessarily love. It wouldn't work out, she told herself soberly. She would go home just as quickly as she could, and after a suitable interval, write to him.

The subject of her thoughts opened the door at that moment, gave her a shrewd glance and said carelessly: 'That's right, leave that thing—go and get your coat, there's a good girl—I've only one patient to see and I shan't be more than ten minutes.' He went away again without waiting for her to answer him.

She was a little longer than that, though, because she met Juffrouw Naald on the stairs, and that good lady, apprised of the news of her departure, wanted to talk about it. Cressida didn't understand every word which was said, but she did gather that she would be missed, and that the housekeeper hoped that she would be back before very long. She ended by saying something which Cressida could understand very well. 'Poor Doctor van der Teile!'

So his Naaldtje knew about Monique too; Cressida made a sympathetic murmur and added in her fragmental Dutch: 'I have to hurry—the doctor is waiting for me.' She smiled at the older woman. 'I shall miss you too,' she managed, and then flew up the rest of the stairs because if she had stayed one minute longer she would have burst into tears and cast herself on Juffrouw Naald's comfortable bosom.

But she was careful not to let any of her feelings show as they drove to Groningen. Indeed, she matched her companion's friendly manner, discussing the prospect of Doctor van Blom's book being a success, the chance of snow for Christmas, the possibility of her getting a Ward Sister's post at the

Royal General ... she wasn't sure how the conversation had got around to that, but somehow it had, and Giles was pinning her down to answers she didn't want to give, and bewildering her too, for hadn't he, only a short time ago, asked her to marry him? Now he was suggesting that she should carve herself a career ...

'Of course, if you should decide to marry me, you wouldn't work,' said Giles, uncannily answering her unspoken questions for her. 'I've more than enough money to indulge your every whim and bring up a family besides.' He uttered this information in such a matter-of-fact voice that she found herself asking: 'Oh, do you like children? So do I —I think a large family would be super, provided one could educate them and clothe them decently and give them a start in life.'

The doctor thought fleetingly of his considerable wealth and smiled. 'Oh, I think that could be managed.' He was still very casual. 'I have some money of my own as well as what I earn, you know, and my home is big enough to house a dozen. Besides, I have a charming house in the country, as well as the farm—so convenient for holidays; children hate hotels.'

'Oh, yes, I remember ...' Cressida stopped; the conversation was getting out of hand and was, in fact, quite absurd. They were talking about holidays with the children, just as though they were already married and with a family to plan for. She asked hurriedly: 'Where exactly is your other house?'

He gave no sign that he had noticed her effort to change the subject. 'Close to the river Vecht. The garden runs down to the water and there's a small landing stage. When I was a small boy Beeker took me fishing—that was after the war had ended, of course—our houses were confiscated during the occupation and we had to share a flat with my grandmother.'

'You were a very little boy—did you realize what was going on?'

'Lord, yes. I was four or five when my father was arrested—I remember that he left me in charge until his return.'

Cressida sat silent, getting rid of the lump in her throat. 'He must have been a rather splendid man,' she said at last.

'He was—he was a fine doctor, too.'

'Did you never wish to be anything else but a doctor?'

He looked surprised. 'No—what else could I be? There have been doctors in the family for generations, it was in my blood, I suppose.'

He slowed the car as they reached the outskirts of the city. 'Would you like to do your shopping first? I've a couple of patients to see. Oh—I'll get my secretary to book you in on a flight tomorrow. Morning or afternoon?'

Cressida considered. 'Well, I'll have to spend the night in London if I'm going to the publisher's and the agency. Could I go in the morning, but not at crack of dawn? I've a friend at the Royal General who'll put me up—I can go on to Aunt Emily's some time during the next day.'

'Just as you like.' His voice was placid, even a little uninterested, she considered peevishly. If he intended to propose again, he would have to be very earnest about it . . . but of course, he wouldn't; the sooner she went the better, especially as he had shown very little interest in her departure. Her thoughts were broken as he turned into a quiet side street and stopped, leaned across to open her door and said: 'Can you be at the hospital in a couple of hours? Ask for me at the porter's lodge.'

She nodded and got out and the Bentley slid away at once. Probably he was late.

Cressida had spent very little of her earnings; she thought with satisfaction of the guldens in her purse and made a beeline for the shops. Something for Aunt Emily, something for Helen, the girl she would be staying the night with; a gift for old Mrs Oakes at the Post Office in the village, because she had always longed to go abroad and never had, and some small keepsake for herself.

She found a charming little silver dish for her aunt as well as some thick, highly coloured knitted gloves, chocolates for Helen, and a Delft blue candlestick and its matching candle for Mrs Oakes and for herself an exquisite little flower miniature. For the doctors she bought ballpoints in vivid colours, for it was a standing joke with the three of them that neither of them could ever find a pen and they always needed to borrow hers. And when her purchases were made there was still time to look around the dress shops and admire their contents. Expensive, Cressida thought, but just the kind of things she would have liked to buy for herself. However, she had spent a good deal more money than she had anticipated, and she might be out of a job for a week or more when she got back; there was very little in her account in England and she would have to be careful, for although Doctor van Blom had paid her return fare she still had the train journey to Dorset to pay for. She turned her back on the pretty clothes and prudently confined her shopping to an elegant headscarf, then made her way to the hospital before she should be further tempted.

Perhaps the porter had been warned of her coming, for he came to meet her as she went in, called to one of her underlings, and waved her on to follow the man with a friendly smile. They went along a great many passages and up and own several small staircases before her guide stopped before a big double door and opened it for her to go through. She found herself in a wide corridor with a number of doors on either side of it and glass doors at its end through which she could see a ward. She turned round to ask the porter if he had made a mistake in bringing her there, but he had gone, and she stood uncertainly, wondering what she should do.

But not for long; a tall, well-built girl in nurse's uniform shot out of a nearby door and advanced to meet her. 'Miss Bingley? We are warned that you come—come with me, if you please.'

Cressida went, thankful that someone knew

where she was. The girl threw open another door and invited her in with a wave of her hand, then shut it behind her. Giles was sitting at the desk under the window, and he got up as she came to a halt.

'Hullo—I've been held up, I'm afraid; I asked them to send you up here while I get finished.'

He pushed the one other chair in the room forward and motioned her to sit down and then spoke into the intercom.

'I've arranged for Zuster Metz to show you round, if you would like that. I'll be through very shortly.'

Zuster Metz was small and round and bustling. She took charge of Cressida, speaking in a mixture of Dutch and bad English and making up for it by the warmth of her manner. 'Women's Medical,' she explained, as she led her from the room. 'Thirty beds and they are always filled. Doctor van der Teile has ten of them—chests.'

She raced into the ward, still talking, finding time to address the patients as they went round and at the same time giving Cressida a précis of their conditions, the number of beds in the hospital, the hours of duty, the number of nurses she had working on the ward, the food served in the hospital canteen, and lastly, the doctor's manifold perfections.

Cressida, her ears ringing, assimilated this information as best she might, thankful that it was only necessary to nod and smile and say yes and no and really every now and then to satisfy the dear soul. She arrived back at the office feeling slightly bewildered, and met Giles' amused look as he got to his feet. 'I'm sure you found that most interesting,' he observed smoothly, and thanked Zuster Metz. 'Shall we go?'

Cressida added her thanks to his and Zuster Metz bubbled her pleasure at meeting her, her hopes to see her again and best wishes for her journey to England into a rigmarole of Dutch and English, as she trotted to the door with them.

'A chatterbox,' commented Giles, as they went down the stairs, 'but one of the best nurses I have had the pleasure of working with.'

Cressida nodded. 'Oh, I know just what you mean,' she agreed seriously. 'She would talk you back to health and strength whether you wanted it or not.' She smiled at him. 'I liked her—and thank you for letting me see the ward.'

He stopped in the middle of the staircase the better to address her. 'I find myself anxious to show you every aspect of my life,' he told her, a remark which took her so much by surprise that she said 'Oh!' in a startled voice and tripped up on a step. He put out a hand and caught her tidily and set her on her feet again, and then didn't take the hand away. His arm felt very pleasant across her shoulder; she stifled an urge to tell him that she loved him as they walked side by side out to the Bentley.

Beeker opened the door as they arrived at his house and Cressida exclaimed: 'However does he know? He always seems to open the door at exactly the right moment.'

'It's an instinct—he prides himself on it; if I

sneak in by the side door I am subjected to reproachful looks for the rest of the day.' He opened the car door and helped her out. 'Come inside and say goodbye to Mama.'

He was being far too cheerful about it, thought Cressida crossly, as they went into the lovely old house; almost as though he were glad she was going. She said austerely: 'You haven't told me if you were able to get me a seat on the plane.'

Giles had thrown off his car coat and given his bag to Beeker, who was holding it as though it contained the Crown Jewels. 'Didn't I? There's a seat for you on the midday plane—you'll be in London in plenty of time to reach your friend during the afternoon.' He took her coat and flung it on top of his own, and started across the hall with a hand under her elbow. 'Doctor van Blom is driving you to the airport.'

Her disappointment was so great that she couldn't speak for a moment, then she managed: 'How kind, but there's really no need ... I could ...'

'Walk? take a bus? hire a taxi? Don't be silly, Cressy.' He had opened a door at the back of the hall as he was speaking and stood aside for her to go into the room beyond. She hadn't been there before. It was smaller than the sitting-room but extremely elegantly furnished, with a bright fire burning in the steel fireplace, and rose-coloured curtains to shut out the winter nights. But now the sun was shining in a watery kind of way, highlighting the pastel colours of the carpet, giving a gloss to the rosewood tables and davenport against one wall, and

163

depth to the blues and greens and pinks of the chair covers. A pretty room and, surprisingly, an excellent background for Mevrouw van der Teile, sitting in one of the more substantial chairs, gowned in sapphire blue velvet, her hair beautifully dressed, her commanding features skilfully made up. She looked up from her embroidery as they went in and said in vibrant tones: 'How nice, my dears—I do so appreciate young people sparing their time to talk to an old woman.'

Her son gave a shout of laughter, kissed her fondly and begged her not to talk rubbish. 'I've brought Cressida to wish you goodbye.'

His mother, just for a moment, looked very like her son at his most bland. 'So soon? My dear child, I had hoped that I would have had many more visits from you before you returned home. However, I daresay that you wish to go back to England—you have plans, perhaps?' She snipped a strand of silk with deliberation. 'You intend to marry?'

Cressida was shocked into a startled: 'Me? Marry? Oh, no! I'm going to get another job.' She avoided the doctor's eye.

'You have never had a proposal of marriage?' asked Mevrouw van der Teile with ruthless charm. 'You surprise me, you are such a very pretty girl.'

'Thank you.' Cressida, whose manners were nice even when harassed, managed to keep her voice matter-of-fact. 'I have had the chance of getting married a few times, only I didn't want to.'

'You are not against marriage?' inquired her in-

terrogator relentlessly. She added in vibrant tones:
'Family life—children...'

'No, of course not, Mevrouw, only it wouldn't do
with the wrong man, would it?'

Mevrouw van der Teile's voice rang out with
the clarity and resonance of Big Ben; for someone
as ill as she had been, she had made a remarkable recovery. 'But perhaps you have found the
right man?'

Cressida, sitting in a little button-back chair,
looked at her hands lying so quietly in her lap and
tried to decide what to say. She could bring the
conversation to a speedy conclusion by saying that
yes, she had; he was sitting there, in the wing-
backed chair next to his mother. On the other hand
she could tell the lady to mind her own business.
There must be a safe, middle-of-the-road answer, if
only she could think of it. Giles thought of it for
her: 'I'll wager the Bentley against one of your
hairpins that you never breathed a word to a soul
once you had set your sights on Father.'

She chuckled richly. 'Indeed, I did not. Cressida,
you must forgive me for being a rude old woman.'

'Oh, but you're not, indeed you're not. It's kind
of you to take an interest...' She caught the doctor's eye and saw that he was smiling faintly and
because of that she added briskly: 'I'm quite looking forward to getting a Ward Sister's post.'

'What a terrible waste!' declared her hostess, and
before she could enlarge on that, Giles remarked
carelessly: 'Oh, but she will make a splendid Sister,
especially when she has had a few years' experience.'

His voice sounded so silky that Cressida knew that he didn't mean a word of it. All the same it annoyed her so much that she suggested gracefully that she should be going. 'Packing and so on,' she explained, and was surprised that when she took her leave, the elder lady kissed her with warm affection. Beeker slid into the hall too, and wished her, rather gloomily, a pleasant journey, and Barker licked her hand, his whiskered face the picture of doggy gloom. Only the doctor seemed unaffected by her departure. Indeed, in the car, driving fast back to his partners' house, he remarked cheerfully:

'Well, now you have the whole afternoon in which to pack, for from the tone of your voice just now, I can only conclude that you have a mountain of luggage, and I have no doubt that the so on, whatever that may be, will take time, too.' He added in the mildest of voices: 'If you hadn't sounded so urgent, I would have invited you to lunch.'

She glanced suspiciously at him, but his profile was as calm as usual. All the same, she suspected that he was laughing at her. 'It isn't the amount of packing there is to be done, there are—there are other things . . .'

'Yes, you said so, dear girl. "And so on". I wouldn't presume to argue.'

They were rounding the square by now; in another few minutes Cressida would have to say goodbye. She watched him get out of the car and come round and open her door. He had never looked more placid and, annoyingly, amused. She bounced out of the Bentley and up to the front door, and had her hand on the knob when it was opened from the other side by Juffrouw Naald, who broke into instant, urgent speech the moment she saw the doctor. They were all inside, with the door shut against the cold, before he explained.

'There is a patient Doctor Herrima wants me to see immediately, Cressida. I'm going at once—tell Doctor van Blom I'll be telephoning him, will you?'

He patted her rather absent-mindedly on the shoulder, kissed Juffrouw Naald on her cheek and went out again, leaving Cressida to take off her hat and coat and presently go to the dining-room and lunch with Doctor van Blom.

She didn't want anything to eat; food choked her, but the kind man sitting opposite her would only get anxious if she didn't pretend to eat. She swallowed whatever it was on her plate and tried not to think that she wasn't going to see Giles again, for of course he didn't really want to marry her— it had been his first reaction against Monique; perhaps he had been looking for an opportunity to tell her that, and now Providence had stepped in and he had been able to go away without any of the embarrassments of saying goodbye.

She packed her things after lunch, tied the typescript up securely and then went for a walk before driving Doctor van Blom on his afternoon round. There had been no sign of Doctor Herrima and certainly none of Giles, and by evening she was so depressed that nothing would have been nicer than to go to bed and have a good cry, but Doctor Her-

rima came in a few minutes before dinner and revealed that they had laid on a special feast as it
was her last night with them, with the pick of
Juffrouw Naald's special dishes and more champagne. So Cressida ate and drank and laughed,
greatly helped by the champagne, and went to bed a
good deal later than usual, determined to sleep,
but despite her best efforts, she lay awake for most
of the remaining night.

They left in plenty of time in the morning, which
was a good thing, for Doctor van Blom drove no
more than a steady thirty miles an hour all the way
to Groningen, and once in the city, slowed to a
walking pace. Cressida was so engrossed in observ-
ing her companion's funereal driving that it wasn't
until they were at the hospital and trundling sedately across its forecourt that she cried: 'Doctor van
Blom, we've gone the wrong way—it's the airport ...'

'Hours to spare,' grunted her companion. 'In a
car of this power, we can reach the airport in
minutes. Got someone to see.'

She followed him inside because he asked her to,
although she hadn't the faintest idea why. It wasn't
until they were in the lift, on their way to the fifth
floor, that she turned to look at her companion
with some suspicion. 'Isn't the fifth Medical?' she
wanted to know. 'That's where G—Doctor van der
Teile has his beds.'

The lift stopped and she was bustled out. 'Quite
right, my dear,' agreed her companion as he hur-

ried her down the corridor and in through the door at the end.

Giles was at the desk once more, looking remote, composed, and exactly as an eminent physician should look. He put down his pen and got up as they went in, and stopped looking like a physician, eminent or otherwise. 'Ah,' he said with satisfaction, 'sooner than I expected—you must have driven fast, Karel.' There was no trace of sarcasm in his voice.

His partner looked suitably modest. 'Fast enough, Giles, fast enough. Well, I'll go and see that patient of ours—be back in a few minutes—mustn't miss that flight.'

After he had gone Giles came round the desk and took Cressida's hand in his. 'I couldn't let you go without saying *tot ziens*,' he told her. 'Did you get all that packing done?'

It really wasn't fair; seeing him again was like reopening an old wound; she had steeled herself to go, and now here he was, stirring everything up again. 'Yes, thank you.'

'Your friend will meet you?'

She was surprised. 'No. I'll get a bus from the Air Terminal.'

He nodded, frowning faintly. 'You have money enough?'

'Yes, thank you.'

He stopped frowning and smiled. 'We're not making much headway, are we? Will you tell me something, Cressy?'

She stared at his tie, his waistcoat, up as far as his chin. 'What do you want to know?' she asked.

'Why are you going back to England? Oh, not all the sound reasons you have given us—the real reason.'

She might just as well tell him, she decided tiredly—indeed, it might snap off the thread of their uneasy relationship. She made herself look at him and said in a clear voice: 'I love you, Giles, but you don't love me. That's why I'm going.'

His hand gripped hers so hard that she winced with the pain, then the door opened and Zuster Metz and Doctor van Blom came in together.

'Miss Bingley,' she exclaimed happily, 'how nice that you come again. I have asked Doctor van Blom to stay for coffee, but he says that he has no time at all—and now I hope that you will excuse me if I speak to Doctor van der Teile on an urgent matter—a patient, you understand.'

It must have been urgent, Giles listened to what she had to say, and without a word or a look, followed her out.

Cressida had no idea how she got to the airport. Presumably she had answered any remarks Doctor van Blom had made on the way, for he hadn't asked if anything was wrong, and as she hadn't seen her poor white face, she was unaware that he, after one glance at her, had concluded that there was nothing that he could say, anyway. Only when her flight was called and she put out a hand to shake his did he suddenly lean forward and kiss her gently on the cheek.

She didn't allow herself to think of anything at all on the flight, and London was busy and bustling enough to keep her thoughts busy too until she arrived at her friend's flat. Somehow the evening passed and strangely enough she slept, to wake the next morning, feeling as though her inside had frozen and would never be warm again, but the day had to be got through; she helped tidy the flat, said goodbye to her friend, went to the publishers and then caught the first train she could to Weymouth.

She hadn't told her aunt at what time she would arrive and took an extravagant taxi out to the village, to find that lady in the little kitchen, potting mincemeat. The homely sight was too much for Cressida. She dropped her case, flung herself at her aunt and burst into tears. Presently she sniffed and said: 'Oh, Aunt Emily, it's so nice to be home!'

Her aunt smiled at her. She knew that that wasn't what Cressida meant to say, but it would do for the present. Later on, perhaps, she would be told what had happened to make her niece's face so white and pinched.

CHAPTER NINE

BEING back in Aunt Emily's little house should have helped Cressida, but it didn't. Giles' face slid between everything she looked at and when she closed her eyes, there he was, beneath the lids. Besides, his voice was always in her ears, so that her aunt was forced to repeat herself on several occasions and then inquire anxiously if her niece was getting deaf. Cressida, denying this for the tenth time at least, very nearly a week after she had returned, offered to do the shopping by way of placating her aunt and went off briskly to the village stores. The little shop was nicely full and Mr Dent, the owner, was looking a little harassed, but her entry proved to be just what he needed, for two or three of his more impatient customers were pleasantly diverted at the sight of her, and engaged her in conversation until it was their turn to be served. Which left Cressida alone, finally, reading from her aunt's list, and having a chat with Mr Dent at the same time.

'I can't say as foreign parts suits 'ee, Miss Bingley,' he observed in his soft Dorset voice. 'It'll 'eve to be corned beef, I'm right out of cooked 'am—as I were saying, pale 'ee be, 'ee was pale a while back when the Reverend and your mother died, but that were natural—I mean to say ... Didn't 'ee like it in Holland?'

'Oh, yes,' said Cressida brightly; after a few days in the village she knew exactly the questions to expect. 'Amsterdam was lovely, though I worked in the north of Holland—for a doctor, you know.'

Of course he knew. In a village so small, everyone knew everything, not because they were curious, but because they were a close-knit community, sincerely interested in each other. Mr Dent looked knowing. 'Any 'andsome young men over there?' he asked, and added: 'It'll 'ave to be Rich Tea biscuits ...'

'Oh, yes, there were,' said Cressida chattily, 'but the doctor I worked for was quite elderly.' She paused. 'He had two partners, though.' Giles' face was so clear before her eyes as she spoke that she looked round, half expecting to see him in the shop too.

She took her groceries and walked back up the high-banked lane to the cottage, Giles' massive shade stalking beside her. She would have to stop being such a fool, she told herself sternly. Tomorrow she would go to London and take the first job the agency offered, and start looking around for a hospital job. In fact, she could go to the Royal General too and see if there was anything ...

She went in through the back door, took off her anorak, hung it behind the door and went into the kitchen, where she unpacked her basket, called up the stairs to her aunt that she was back and would start getting their midday meal ready, and went to the sink.

The postman had been, but there were no letters

for her; apart from a brief line from Doctor van Blom, which had contained no word of Giles, she had had no news. 'Out of sight, out of mind,' she said bitterly. 'If only I had held my tongue—what a fool I was to tell him that I loved him ... like a silly lovesick girl.' She picked up a potato and began to peel it with ferocity. 'I hate him,' she said loudly. 'I hate him—I never want to see him again!'

'Try telling him that to his face,' said the doctor from the door behind her, and she whizzed round, dropped the knife with a clatter and let the potato roll across the floor between them.

'How long have you been there?' she demanded, joy at seeing him quite swamped by the fear that he must have heard what she had been saying.

'You didn't want to see me again,' he told her. 'Why? Have I missed any more observations?'

She ignored that. 'I've been here a week, I thought ...'

He smiled at her and her heart turned over. 'That I should have written. My dear girl, a letter wouldn't have done at all; there are some questions ... You told me that you loved me and in the same breath you declared that I didn't love you and that was why you were returning here, and all this at a time when it was impossible for me to answer you or even discover exactly what it was you meant.'

Cressida eyed him across the little room. His face wore its usual bland expression, but she had the feeling that he wasn't bland at all. Perhaps he had come to tell her that she had done the right thing, that he hadn't been serious about wanting to marry her, perhaps he was going to tell her that he was interested in her after all, that he might manage to dismiss Monique from his mind . . .

She drew a deep breath. 'Monique——' she began, and saw his frown. 'You were in love with her, weren't you—still are, for all I know. It must have been ghastly for you when you discovered that she had married someone else. I suppose that's why you asked me to marry you—you had to rush off and ask the first girl you met to pay her out . . .' She sighed. 'I expect that's a natural reaction . . .' She looked at him and although there was no change in his expression, she took a step backwards.

'You really think that?' His voice was very quiet, but he spoke bitingly. 'You thought that of me— you didn't tell me.' His eyes were very cold.

Despite her efforts to stay calm and matter-of-fact, two tears welled up and trickled slowly down her cheeks. 'I thought it was true,' she mumbled, 'and—and you never said that you loved me—you haven't said it now . . .'

His icy stare sent her two shades paler even though he remained silent. 'Your attitude towards me was hardly encouraging,' he pointed out, 'and when, just once or twice, it was, you were in the throes of 'flu or I was ringed round with my work.'

She showed sudden temper. 'Oh, indeed—and what was I supposed to do? Do you imagine . . .' She choked, blew her nose defiantly, and began again. 'I thought you loved Monique—I saw you together one day at Doctor van Blom's. You were in the sitting-room together—you had your arms round her . . .'

He said with a studied patience which set her teeth on edge: 'Monique was married to a lifelong friend. We went to school together, he and I, and then to medical school, and eventually he held a consultant's post in Groningen. He died of C A three years ago, and I promised him that I would keep an eye on Monique, and she promised him that if ever she should remarry, she would first of all tell me; you see, Wim wanted it to be the right man; Monique is impetuous and she has a good deal of money. He hoped that she would seek my advice. And as for seeing us together'—he stopped to think, 'ah, yes, that day we came up to your room and you had been crying. Peeping, were you, Cressida? Not like you, I should have said ... Monique was unhappy, I thought she was still grieving for Wim and I was comforting her as I would have comforted anyone, man, woman or child. And why I should be forced to make this lengthy explanation I cannot imagine.' He went on curtly, 'The trouble with you is that you allow your imagination to run away with you.'

He still hadn't said that he loved her, and somehow that mattered far more than knowing that he didn't love Monique. She was prompted to say with a fine disregard for the truth, 'Perhaps I do, but not any more I won't—you've made it plain that I imagined that I loved you, haven't you? And I'm sorry you found it necessary to explain so much of your private life to me—and don't dare answer that, for I can see that you're in a towering temper. Well, so am I, and I hope that I may never have to set eyes on you again!'

She heard herself utter the words with something like horror, and regretted them the moment they were out of her mouth, but it was too late. The eyes that she had found so cold were blazing now. He had turned and gone through the door, closing it quietly behind him, and her breathless, squeaky 'Giles,' was uttered to an empty room.

She should have run after him, but her legs refused to move at first; by the time she had wrenched the door open, darted down the passage and reached the front of the cottage, the Bentley's elegant tail was disappearing round a bend in the lane. It was silly to stand there calling his name; even if he had heard it, he wasn't going to come back.

Cressida went back indoors, and Aunt Emily, coming downstairs, paused to ask her if she felt all right. 'You're as white as a sheet, child,' she observed. 'Have you had a tiff with that nice-looking man who just plunged out of the front door?'

Cressida let out a wail and rushed into the kitchen and shut the door, and her aunt, being a sensible woman, went into the sitting-room and picked up her knitting. It was high time that lunch was prepared, but it was only too obvious to her that her niece, at the moment, had no interest in food. She rummaged round in her workbag and found a half-eaten block of chocolate and nibbled at it philosophically while she waited for Cressida to reappear.

Which she did after some twenty minutes, pale

and red-eyed and subdued. She helped get their meal, laid the table, fed the cats and then sat pecking at her lunch, making bright remarks about nothing in particular, until Aunt Emily put down her knife and fork and said firmly: 'You had better tell me about it, Cressy. Who knows, I might be able to help you.'

'No one can help,' Cressida said a little wildly. 'I'll never see him again. You see, there was a muddle—a misunderstanding—I thought he was going to marry someone else and he wasn't...'

'He wanted to marry you?'

'He said so, and he came this morning—and I don't really know why we had to quarrel. It was me, I suppose.' She sniffed. 'He got very angry and I told him I never wanted to see him again, and he went...'

'A very natural reaction,' said her aunt comfortably. 'Men, especially men in love, are sometimes most unreasonable. What do you intend doing?'

'Well, I'll have to go after him, won't I? He's very pig-headed.'

'But you love him, Cressy.' Aunt Emily pushed back her chair. 'He looked rather super,' she remarked surprisingly. 'I had a good look from my bedroom window. Now there's a timetable somewhere—the one you had ... it's too late to go today, but if you left in the morning you should get there by the evening.' She had found the timetable and was leafing through it. 'Yes, here we are: train to London and then down to Heathrow—let me see, a couple of hours for the flight—there's one to

Groningen in the early afternoon—will that do? Wait a minute while I write the times down, then you'd better go to the Post Office and telephone.'

There was a seat on an afternoon flight. Cressida booked it with much the same sensation as she always felt when she booked a dental appointment; something which had to be done and which she didn't look forward to. Giles would be angry, with that nasty cold rage which froze her very bones, but at least she could say she was sorry and if she felt brave enough, she could ask him if he loved her ... Carried away on a flood of high resolve, she hurried back to the cottage to fling a change of clothes into a case and count her money.

It was snowing when Cressida arrived in Groningen and she had to wait a little while for a taxi. She was by now tired, hungry and filled with such impatience to get to Giles as quickly as possible that the hunger and tiredness didn't matter. When at length she got her taxi, she sat on the edge of the seat, quivering with excitement. In a very short time now she would see him, and despite the various speeches she had rehearsed during her journey, she still had no idea what she was going to say to him—perhaps she would know when she saw him.

The house looked welcoming as she got out of the taxi, the big windows lighted against the dark outside, the chandelier shining through the elaborate transom over the great door. She reached for the knocker and gave it a determined thump.

Beeker opened the door, beamed a surprised welcome and stood aside to allow her to enter. He picked up her overnight bag and set it down on one of the hall tables with the air of someone who expected her to stay, and the small gesture gave her courage to ask. 'The doctor? Could I see him, Beeker?'

He gave her a look of regret. 'The doctor is at the hospital, giving the last of a series of lectures to the post-graduates. He will not return for some time, Miss—indeed, there was some talk of him spending the remainder of the evening with the Dean. I had orders not to wait up.' He looked at her more closely. 'You're tired, Miss Bingley. Allow me to get you a light meal and in the meantime Ineke will get a room ready for you.'

Cressida gave him a distracted look. A fine thing it would be if Giles refused to see her and she expected to spend the night at his home. 'I haven't time,' she told him urgently. 'I'm going down to the hospital—I know where it is. If you would please take care of my bag until I get back? I—I don't expect to stay here, but I've nowhere to put it for the moment.'

Beeker received this news with an impassive face. 'We shall hope to see you shortly, miss,' he assured her, and opened the door to show her out. 'Let me call a taxi for you, miss.'

Cressida paused. 'It's only a few minutes if I go down that funny little passage on the other side of the canal, isn't it? I'll walk, I'm sure I can remember the way.' She remembered to smile at him. 'Thank you, Beeker.'

She almost ran, despite common sense telling her that to arrive all breathless and worked up wasn't going to help her at all. On the other hand, suppose the lecture was finished and Giles had already gone? What was she to do? Follow him to the Dean's house? Go back to his home and accept his un-offered hospitality? Both were unthinkable. She flung common sense to the winds, and ran through the narrow passage between the houses which would bring her within a stone's throw of the hospital.

She hadn't stopped to think what she would do when she got there; it was surprisingly easy, as a matter of fact, for when she asked the porter on duty: 'Doctor van der Teile?' he called at once to a younger man, and put her in his charge. Cressida hurried along several passages and up and down a stair or two before he opened a quite small door rather cautiously and with finger to lip, motioned her to enter.

The lecture hall was filled to overflowing with medical students, post-graduates, house doctors and a sprinkling of well-dressed gentlemen in the front rows—fellow consultants, probably. She took a providential empty seat just by the door, high up at the top of the hall, and fastened her eyes on the platform. Giles was there, in the middle, standing behind a desk. There was a pile of notes before him, but he didn't seem to be using them. He was looking around his audience as he spoke, and she was thankful that the lighting was on the dim side. Besides, she was a long way from him.

She sat listening to his deep voice, not understanding more than a word here and there, but that didn't matter, just to be near him was enough for the moment. She became aware that she was very tired and a little woolly in the head; she should really use this time to make a few sensible plans, but none came, so she just sat, listening to his incomprehensible words and enjoying them. They lulled her to a tranquillity she hadn't enjoyed for some time now, so that she was quite surprised when his voice ceased and there was an outburst of applause. Should she whip through the door and wait for him in the entrance hall—and perhaps miss him? Or should she wait for the audience to go and make her way to the platform? She dithered too long and the people around started to move away, so that the platform was obscured for a moment. Cressida got up slowly, still undecided, and saw the platform was empty. 'Fool!' she admonished herself fiercely, and two young women doctors paused to stare at her on their way out.

The door beside her opened and Giles whisked her through it without a word; they had negotiated the various passages and steps, crossed the entrance hall and were actually by the Bentley before she had found her voice. 'You couldn't have seen me.'

'Of course I saw you—the only fur hat in the place, and coming in late, too. Get in.'

His manner was non-committal, but she did as she was told, wondering if she had made—and was about to make—a terrific fool of herself. The awkwardness of her situation struck her forcibly and gave her something to worry about as he drove back to his house without saying another word. Only as Beeker opened the door to them did he have something to say, and that was to his houseman and in his own language.

Cressida found herself swept into the sitting-room and offered a small armchair by the fire, and: 'Take off your coat,' invited Giles in the polite voice of a careful host, 'Beeker will be bringing coffee in a moment.' He cast her a lightning glance. 'When did you last have something to eat?'

She looked at him vacantly, trying to remember. 'I had coffee and a roll before I got on the plane.'

He crossed the splendid Aubusson carpet and tugged the bell-rope by the hearth and waited until Beeker came. 'Miss Bingley hasn't eaten for hours,' he told him. 'Will you ask Ineke to send something along? Soup and an omelette, perhaps.' He looked across at Cressida. 'Did you bring any luggage with you?'

'I—I asked Beeker to mind it for me, I hope you don't mind—just while I went to the hospital.'

'See that Miss Bingley's things go up to the room she had previously, will you, Beeker?'

It was disconcerting and annoying too that Giles had taken over the situation. 'No,' she said suddenly, 'I don't want to stay here.' She added belatedly: 'Thank you. You weren't pleased to see me—there's no reason why you should be, I suppose. I couldn't possibly stay.'

The doctor lifted an eyebrow at Beeker, who slid from the room with a blank face which became wreathed in satisfied smiles the moment he had shut the door behind him.

'Explain?' suggested Giles, his voice very gentle.

She got up and walked to the window and looked out into the quiet dark street; it would be so much easier to talk if she didn't look at him. 'I had to see you,' she began, 'to tell you that I was sorry. I don't deserve to be forgiven, but it was all lies, of course. I love you, I told you that, and it was very silly of me, too, but—well, it's made my love seem a very poor thing, hasn't it—not worth bothering about.' She swung round and made herself look at him. 'I won't stay here—I can't!'

Giles was standing with his back to the fire, his hands in his pockets. 'You will and you can,' he assured her affably. 'My poor darling, muddle-headed goose, do you really suppose that I could stop loving you just because you flew into a rage? I believe I know you better than you know yourself, Cressy. Do you think that I would have walked away and left you if I hadn't been sure that you would come to me? But I had to leave you, my darling, to make up your own mind once you discovered that you trusted me as well as loved me. And that I loved you.'

Cressida sniffed. 'You didn't speak ... I'd thought of all the things I was going to say and when you didn't even say hullo, I couldn't remember one of them.'

He had left the fireplace and was standing close to her. 'If I say hullo now would that help you to remember them?'

184

A tear sparkled on her lashes and she wiped it away impatiently with the back of her hand. 'Only that I'm sorry.'

She was unprepared for his sudden swoop and the long lingering kiss he gave her. 'That will do for a start,' he told her, and sat her down again as Beeker came in with a tray, which he arranged carefully on a little papier-mâché table, painted and inlaid with mother-of-pearl, beside her chair. There was a coffee pot and cups, delicate little sandwiches, a covered cup of soup, strips of buttered toast and a garnished omelette on a silver dish. Cressida eyed it with pleasure, although it seemed quite wrong for a girl to want her supper just as her most romantic dreams seemed about to come true. Giles poured coffee for them both and said: 'Drink your soup, my darling girl, and polish off those odds and ends—I don't want you fainting on my hands.'

She smiled a little shyly at him then and fell to, while he sat in his great chair watching her. She was finishing the last morsel of toast when he said, half laughing, 'And now, if you have finished your supper ...' and got out of his chair and plucked her out of hers to hold her close.

'The days have been very long,' he told her, 'and I wanted to come to you, and then suddenly there you were, staring at me over all those heads. It's a wonder that I finished my lecture, for I wanted to leap off that platform and pick you up in my arms ...' He pulled her a little closer. 'I could think of nothing to say when I opened that door and you were still standing there—I was so afraid that you would be gone.' He kissed her slowly. But perhaps there is no need to say anything, just I love you, Cressy, and will you marry me as soon as possible.'

She looked up into his face. 'You're quite sure? You're not saying it just because I came running after you ...' If she had had more to say, she would have had no opportunity to say it, and presently, getting her breath again, she could see that there was no point in saying any more, anyway. She kissed him quickly and observed, 'I may not be very suitable, Giles ...'

She felt him shake with laughter. 'My love, you seemed entirely suitable the moment I set eyes on you, being so dignified about getting lost in Amsterdam, and I've never changed my opinion.'

'Why didn't you tell me that you didn't love Monique?' she asked him.

'You didn't ask me, dearest, and it never entered my head to tell you—why should it?'

'Oh,' said Cressida blankly, and then, remembering: 'But you were always so cross—when we went to the clinic you didn't want me to go with you.'

He kissed the top of her head. 'Darling, you must understand that it is a little difficult for a man to be with the girl he loves and not tell her so.'

'Then why didn't you?'

He smiled: 'I had the feeling that you didn't altogether approve of me.'

She smiled back at him. 'Oh, but I do, darling Giles; you could tell me now, if you like.'

Beeker, coming in to remove the tray, slid out again, a smile of intense satisfaction on his chubby face. At last the old house would have a mistress, there would be entertaining, children ... He trotted off kitchenwards, intent on passing on the good news to Ineke.

YOU'LL L♥VE
Harlequin Magazine

for women who enjoy reading fascinating stories of exciting romance in exotic places

SUBSCRIBE NOW!

This is a colorful magazine especially designed and published for the readers of Harlequin novels.

Now you can receive your very own copy delivered right to your home every month throughout the year for only 75¢ an issue.

This colorful magazine is available only through Harlequin Reader Service, so enter your subscription now!

In every issue...

Here's what you'll find:

 a complete, full-length romantic novel...illustrated in color.

 exotic travel feature...an adventurous visit to a romantic faraway corner of the world.

 delightful recipes from around the world...to bring delectable new ideas to your table.

 reader's page...your chance to exchange news and views with other Harlequin readers.

 other features on a wide variety of interesting subjects.

Start enjoying your own copies of Harlequin magazine immediately by completing the subscription reservation form.

Harlequin Reader Service
MPO Box 707,
Niagara Falls, N.Y. 14302

In Canada:
Stratford, Ontario
N5A 6W4

I wish to subscribe to Harlequin magazine beginning with the next issue. I enclose my check or money order for $9.00 for 12 monthly issues.

NAME_____

ADDRESS_____

CITY_____

STATE/PROV._____ ZIP/POSTAL CODE_____

ROM 2095

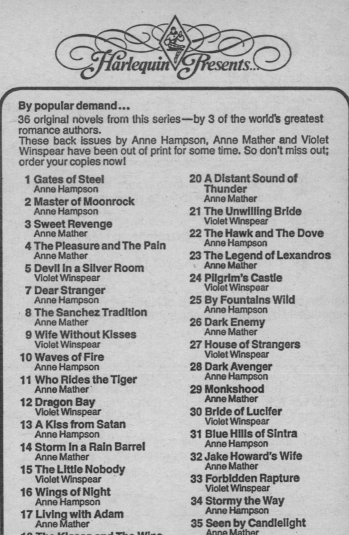

Harlequin Presents...

By popular demand...

36 original novels from this series—by 3 of the world's greatest romance authors.

These back issues by Anne Hampson, Anne Mather and Violet Winspear have been out of print for some time. So don't miss out; order your copies now!

All the above titles are available at 95¢ each. Please use the attached order form to indicate your requirements.

Harlequin Reader Service
ORDER FORM

Mail coupon to:
Harlequin Reader Service,
M.P.O. Box 707,
Niagara Falls, New York 14302

Canadian Residents send to:
Harlequin Reader Service,
Stratford, Ont. N5A 6W4

Please send me by return mail the books that I have checked.
I am enclosing 95¢ for each book ordered.

Please check volumes requested:

☐ 1	☐ 11	☐ 20	☐ 29
☐ 2	☐ 12	☐ 21	☐ 30
☐ 3	☐ 13	☐ 22	☐ 31
☐ 4	☐ 14	☐ 23	☐ 32
☐ 5	☐ 15	☐ 24	☐ 33
☐ 7	☐ 16	☐ 25	☐ 34
☐ 8	☐ 17	☐ 26	☐ 35
☐ 9	☐ 18	☐ 27	☐ 36
☐ 10	☐ 19	☐ 28	☐ 37

Number of books ordered_____ @ 95¢ each = $_____

N.Y. and N.J. residents add appropriate sales tax $_____

Postage and handling = $ _____.25

TOTAL = $_____

NAME _____
(please print)

ADDRESS _____

CITY _____

STATE/PROV. _____ ZIP/POSTAL CODE _____

ROM 2095

Send for your copy today!

The Harlequin Romance Catalog FREE!

Here's your chance to catch up on all the wonderful Harlequin Romance novels you may have missed because the books are no longer available at your favorite booksellers.

Complete the coupon and mail it to us. By return mail, we'll send you a copy of the latest Harlequin catalog. Then you'll be able to order the books you want directly from us.

Clip and mail coupon today.

Harlequin Reader Service
M.P.O. Box 707
Niagara Falls, N.Y. 14302

In Canada:
Harlequin Reader Service
Stratford, Ontario   N5A 6W4

Please send my FREE
Harlequin Romance Catalog!

NAME

ADDRESS

CITY

STATE }
PROV }   ZIP }
          POSTAL CODE }   ROM 2095